THE
FULL CIRCLE

THE
FULL CIRCLE

Stumbling Upon A Sinful Mystery

NAMRATA GUPTA

Srishti
PUBLISHERS & DISTRIBUTORS

SRISHTI PUBLISHERS & DISTRIBUTORS
Registered Office: N-16, C.R. Park
New Delhi – 110 019
Corporate Office: 212A, Peacock Lane
Shahpur Jat, New Delhi – 110 049
editorial@srishtipublishers.com

First published by
Srishti Publishers & Distributors in 2018

10 9 8 7 6 5 4 3 2 1

Printed at Repro Knowledgecast Limited, Thane

To my family,
whose thumbs up every time
I wrote a chapter,
made me write even more.

The Journey Within

The clarity of the light blue sky was marred by numerous white clouds, irregularly shaped, rather enhancing the beauty of the picturesque landscape instead of decreasing it. Quite a juxtaposition of the words 'marring' and 'enhancing', because sometimes the loss of clarity leads to something even more beautiful. Not every time is pin point perfection required. The morning clouds, didn't for a moment, fail to veil that they had a million tiny droplets of water inside them, perfectly and symmetrically arranged to resemble a perfectly asymmetrical structure.

As a man moved along the path with tall trees and lush green gardens on both sides, in his front and at his back, he saw a huge mountain peeping from behind the fog, standing majestically, trying to show itself to the world. The fog wasn't too stubborn so as to not comply with the mountains' demands and in seconds it made way for the mountain to display its intricate, uneven, rocky structure with all its ups and downs, highs and lows. The sight was heavenly! No Photoshop could have created an image so magnificent and glorious.

It was 7:00 a.m., but not too early for the crows to feed on the bread the man had thrown for them. Crows and sparrows tried to mix in their soothing melodies with the calm and peaceful surroundings and were so successful in their endeavours that Munnar became a place which was difficult to leave. They were the untrained artists who seemed better than the trained ones!

The man came down the sloped path and looked for some conveyance to take him to the bus stop. He was soon in the bus, awaiting the commencement of the fourteen-hour long journey that would take him to Chennai from where he would get on the train to Siliguri. With his backpack on his side, the nostalgia of the past three months that he had spent in Kerala crept in.

In these past three months, he had worked as a chef in a resort. Having travelled to various parts of the country and the world, he knew how to prepare different cuisines well. This talent got him a place in the resort which catered to a lot of tourists. Apart from working as a chef, he had also worked at cultural centres as he was aware of different cultures, taught English to people employed in the tourism industry and cab drivers as they needed to have the basic understanding of the language to communicate with tourists from various parts of the world, participated in cultural nights and learnt Kathakali, too.

Being a traveller, he always took something with him from the place he visited and this somehow helped him to give something to his next destination. Giving something was usually in the form of a foreign language like French, German, Bengali and other indigenous languages; or food in the form of different cuisines and snacks available in different parts of the world; or cultural dances or music or random stories of his excursions which people loved to hear; or open photograph exhibitions in parks; or selling some rare commodity found at one place in case of extreme necessity with no other means of survival. But all this was in one sense necessary to survive at an alien place and to save money to travel to another. Nothing exists without the Barter system, but this system of giving and taking wasn't merely a system of exchange; it also brought with itself a plethora of experiences, knowledge, understanding of one's innermost desires, and exploration of one's innermost fears. This made him richer than monetary exchange could. Jobs which required him to stay at one place for a considerable time were of no interest to him; staying didn't define him, constant exploration did.

In the last three months, he had collected a manageable sum of money to allow him to travel to his next destination and eat his bread and butter for some days, just in case finding an occupation got difficult.

While travelling in the bus, the memories of the lakes, beaches, mountains, huts, tree houses, houseboats, boating, forests, elephants, tea estate and backwater, flashed crystal clear in front of his eyes. The sound of the waves, the calmness of the mountains, the sight of newly caught fish, and the rustic life – there was nothing that he had forgotten and neither did he intend to.

The best of his stories were written in the pages of his passport. His life was an endless series of getaways, and not getaways as a means of temporarily escaping the harsh reality to take breaks from work, routine life and monotony. He had inverted this tradition and instead made work, monotony and routines temporary, means to save money for his next journey. He wasn't interested in being a millionaire or gathering glittering gold, or getting a cash rich job. His biggest investments were not kept for future, but for the present. His adventurous life was his investment, the mementos that he collected from the places he visited were his treasure, facing and eliminating his innermost fears were his achievements, and understanding himself was his wealth. The continuous moulding of his self by new encounters and experiences made him more receptive to situations, wiser and more flexible.

He took out sandwiches, which he had got packed from Munnar, from his backpack, and ate them in a jiffy. They satiated his hunger. He leaned himself more towards the window and rested his head exactly where he could feel the soft breeze touching his cheeks. Such a soothing effect did the filled stomach and gentleness of the breeze have on him, that it didn't take him more than a few minutes to fall asleep. There was calmness on his face as he slept with satisfaction; the kind of satisfaction we get on doings things which we really want to do in our life.

Two days had passed since he had left Munnar. It took him almost fifty-four hours to reach Siliguri. From there, he took a cab to reach Darjeeling.

Darjeeling is a place located in the hills. Already weak with his journey of almost fifty-four hours with no adequate intake of food, the man was feeling nauseated. Too proud to admit that, he wanted to quickly reach his destination. Because as a traveller, getting sick of driving up the high sloped mountains was against his code of conduct! After another one-and-a-half hours, he reached Darjeeling.

"Where do you want to go, sir?" asked the cab driver.

"Take me to a good place to eat first, then we'll find some accommodation," he replied.

The cab driver nodded.

The man was really hungry. He would have found an accommodation first, where he could leave his backpack, but he was craving for food, and it became his top-most priority at that time.

The cab driver dropped him in front of a famous restaurant on the Mall Road, 'Hasty Tasty'. Every place has renowned eating joints for tourists, which are mentioned to all the people looking for a food joint. This was one such joint.

He went inside the restaurant and looked for a table. The restaurant was packed with people since it was lunch time. After waiting for ten minutes, he finally found a place to sit. In those ten minutes, he had placed his order, 'Order number thirty-seven'. The restaurant had many cuisines to choose from – North Indian, South Indian, Chinese, Italian, Arabian, etc. He had ordered an Indian *thali*, noodles and a brownie shake. He was too tired to get into the ordering line again, so without caring about his stomach being full after eating the main course, he ordered noodles at that time only. He could always get it packed, he thought.

After having his food, he came out of the restaurant and called the cab driver. While waiting for his cab, he roamed around the area a bit and found an advertisement posted on the door of another restaurant.

It read, 'Room Available under Four Thousand Rupees, for boys and girls.' The address was written below. When his cab arrived, he showed the advertisement to the driver and asked to drop him at that place.

"How was the food, sir?" the driver asked.

"It was good," he replied, continuing, "Do you have any idea about the house we're going to? How is the area? The room? The people? "

"The locality is good. The people are very nice. I haven't seen the room though!" the driver replied.

"Okay," the man said.

"This is the house, sir," the driver said, pointing his finger towards the house.

The man got out of the cab, paid the driver, collected his belongings and walked towards the house. The cab driver left.

The Guest

The house looked aesthetic with its yellow and red coloured walls and old school windowpanes. It looked like a rectangle filled with yellow colour and boundaries marked by red. The shed looked beautiful with its crescent shaped surface that enhanced the beauty of the house.

He rang the doorbell. A girl, who looked around twenty-one years old, dressed in a black kurti and black leggings, with hair tied in a bun on the top, opened the door. She was slim, fair, her eyes big and lips pink. No cosmetics could have enhanced the beauty of her face. Her face was perfect without a thing as common as kajal or a lipstick. Her soft pink lips looked like newly blossomed roses; her plain big eyes, her sharp thin nose and her youthful fresh face couldn't be beheld at once. It looked as if she was to be observed for a lifetime, her features to be seen a thousand times over for any imperfections. Her face was to be dwelled at, her eyes were to be read, the share of her nose was to be charted out, the sight of her lips was to be cherished. She was the epitome of natural human beauty that could put all the cosmetic beauty enhancers to shame.

"I saw the advertisement regarding the availability of a room here," the man said.

She nodded.

"Wait here," she said and went inside the house.

She came back after a minute and allowed him to get inside the house.

The man entered the house and saw a woman sitting on a red coloured sofa.

"Please sit," the girl said, pointing towards the seat in front of the lady.

The lady was plump, fair, her hair tied up in a bun, wearing an orange kurta and black leggings.

"So you want a room?" the lady asked.

"Yes," the man replied.

"What's your name?" she asked.

"Aditya," he replied.

"Where are you from?" she asked further.

"Do you intend to ask my hometown? Because there's no particular place I live in," he replied.

"I didn't get you." She looked puzzled.

"I am a traveller. I don't stay at one place for too long. So there's no particular place where I live. I've lived in different parts of the country. But if you ask about my hometown, it's in Madhya Pradesh," he explained.

As he said this, he could see the girl standing beside the lady getting uncomfortable. She looked at him in a manner he had never seen before. A multitude of emotions crossed her face. Her eyes looked helpless and yet they displayed anger.

The man noticed this, but was unable to figure out where he went wrong.

"So what do you do to manage a living?" the lady asked.

"I don't have a profession as such, but I earn by doing small tasks and engaging in different cultural activities," he replied.

"Will you be able to pay our rent?" she questioned.

"Yes. Cent percent. I've lived for years like this. I don't have financial problems of that sort," he replied.

"Show me your identity cards," she said.

He showed her all the cards he had. After going through them, she showed him the room .

The room looked nice with one bed, a cupboard, a study table, a lamp and an attached washroom.

When they came back from the room, the girl had gone to the kitchen.

"Did you like the room?" the lady asked.

"Yes, I did," he replied.

"Okay. So the rent is four thousand rupees for one month, which you'll have to pay in advance before you start living in; this is without food. If you want to include food, you'll have to pay extra," she declared.

"See, I just want one meal per day from you people. The rest I will manage. But I can't say if I would want breakfast or lunch or dinner. I can promise one meal, which could be any of the three. I'll eat whatever is made, that's not an issue," he said.

"Just one meal?" she asked to confirm.

"Yes," he replied.

"I can demand any of the three meals as per my convenience," he added.

"That's fine. So for one meal per day for a month, I'll charge you…umm… one thousand five hundred rupees," she said.

He remained silent.

"See, if you eat outside for a month, I'm sure one meal will not cost you less than that. It will definitely be more. Here, we'll give you whatever you wish to have, rice or chapati, you'll get to choose amongst whatever is made at home," she said.

"And we are not rude people. If you ask us to make something of your choice once or twice, we'll see to it that you are not disappointed," she added.

He smiled and agreed.

"So I have to pay five thousand five hundred rupees in total?" he asked.

"Yes," she replied.

"Right now?" he asked.

"Pay the rent as of now. You can pay for the food at the end of the month," she replied.

"By the way, for how long do you want the room?" she asked.

"One month as of now. We can extend it later, if needed," he replied.

"Alright. We'll provide you with two water jugs every day," she said.

"What if I need more?" he asked.

"We'll see at that time," she replied.

He nodded.

He opened his backpack, took out his wallet and handed over the required sum of money to her. She gave him the keys to his room. He collected his luggage and went inside the room.

The lady went inside the kitchen and asked the girl to keep a jug filled with water in the man's room.

"Why did you agree to keep him in our house?" The girl shouted in frustration.

"Slow, Zinnia!" the lady scolded her.

"You know who he is, mother! Why would you do that to me!" She vent out her frustration.

"You know how difficult it was getting a paying guest. After so long, we have got one. And also, he's here for a month only, as of now! Why don't you forget all that, Zinnia. Haven't we given you enough happiness to make you forget everything that happened?" she cried out.

"No, it's not like that. Mother... Sorry mother. Please forgive me." She apologised, seeing the lady like that.

She quickly poured water into the jug and went inside the rented room. The man was unpacking his luggage. Without looking at him, she kept the glass and jug onto the table and left the room, her head still down. He noticed her manner, but couldn't figure out anything.

After sorting out his belongings and taking adequate rest, he went out to the Mall Road in the evening. He didn't want to waste even a single evening staying inside the house. He looked at the various things, shops, people, games, activities around him and smiled as he walked past them. He had his dinner in the market and came to his room only to sleep.

A small boy of about ten years came to his room, playing with a blue ball while he was preparing to sleep.

"Sid! Sid! Don't go there. Wait!" The girl shouted from behind.

The man smiled on seeing the boy and sat on his knees to talk to him.

"What's your name?" he asked.

"Sid," the boy replied.

"You are our new guest na, uncle?" he added.

"Yes beta," he replied, playing with the boy's ball.

"We are so sorry to disturb you," the girl apologised.

"No, it's alright," he replied.

"Come Sid! You have to sleep now." The girl called out and took him with her.

The next morning, the man came outside the house, dressed up and prepared to explore the city. He was wearing a full sleeves black T-shirt with blue jeans, with a bag on his left shoulder. He saw the girl, hanging out clothes to dry.

"Hi, what's your name?" he asked.

"Zinnia," she replied.

"Nice! Zinnia, actually I wanted to check out some spots in the city today. Could you please tell me how do I commute? And where should I go?" he enquired.

"You can use a private taxi, but that would be expensive. A shared taxi would be cheaper. Otherwise there's the bus and the train," she answered.

"Okay. Where do I get a shared taxi from? Any stand?" he asked.

She went inside the house and brought a slip along.

"Here. You can call him and ask for details."

She said, handing over the slip to him.

"Thanks. And where should I go?" he asked.

"He'll know better. He deals with a lot of tourists." She answered, pointing out to the name in the slip.

"Actually I'm not a tourist. I am a traveller," he said.

"Never mind," she said and got back to her work.

"What do you do, by the way?" he asked.

"Embroidery, sewing… needle work," she answered.

"Okay," he replied.

She went inside the house, not caring about any further questions he might have and he went on to call the owner of the shared taxi.

Impressions

Aditya came back from the tea estates in the evening. He was really interested in knowing about the life of the leaf pickers, the people who take care of the estate, the process of plantation, the difficulties faced and the techniques used for the same, if somebody could lose his life during the plantation process due to steep slopes, and a hundred other queries that kept popping up in his head. But, he wanted the answers from the people who worked there, the locals, the natives and the working women. He wanted to understand and know about their lives, their fears and desires. He didn't want to interact with the owners, the faces, but with the hands, the people who worked.

But since he couldn't speak the language they spoke, he couldn't do that. He had faced this problem even in Munnar because the working people didn't understand Hindi and English – the languages he used. They spoke in their own dialects and regional languages, which he couldn't understand. His language could be understood only by the owners and this blocked his attempts of getting into the intricacies of life of the people working in the tea plantations, from getting a rich wholesome experience and understanding of their lifestyle and kept him at an arm's length from their version of truth.

Dejected, he came out of his room to sit at the door of the house with Zinnia, where she was cutting vegetables for dinner.

"Hi!" he greeted her, sitting by her side.

"Hi!" she replied back, getting up to go inside.

"Where are you going? Hey, listen!" he called out behind her.

She stopped without turning towards him.

He stepped in front of her and asked, "Do you not like my staying here?"

"When did I say that?" she replied.

"You haven't, but your body language does," he said.

"There's nothing like that," she replied, trying to move ahead.

"Did I unknowingly upset you? I am sorry if I did. If you don't like me staying here, I will find some other place and tell nobody the reason for the same." He asserted.

"Why would you do that ? I am not your friend. You don't even know me," she said.

"Because I don't want to make anybody uncomfortable because of me," he replied.

"And would finding a new house be comfortable for you?" she asked back.

"No, it wouldn't be but I don't want to gain my comfort at the expense of someone else's," he replied.

She remained silent for a minute and then answered, "I don't mind you staying here. Don't worry".

"Are you sure?" he confirmed.

"Yes," she replied.

He smiled and asked her if they could chat a little. She agreed and they sat by the door.

"Which language is mostly spoken by the locals here?" he asked her.

"Commonly, people speak Bengali, Nepali and English. There are other languages also like Tibetan and others," she answered.

"Oh, okay!" he said.

"I went to the tea estates today. I wanted to interact with the workers at the plantations, but couldn't, because I don't speak the same language as them," he added.

"Hmm... What did you want to talk about?" she asked.

"Their lives, dreams, work, culture, lifestyle. Knowing about people from different areas and cultures interests me," he answered.

"That's why you are a traveller? And do you have a lot of money to waste? Travelling and doing nothing with your life?" she asked.

"Waste? Who said I'm wasting my money? What makes you say that! Firstly, I am always broke. You are richer than me, trust me. I have only that much money which can help me survive. I'm not a rich guy. Secondly, I'm not wasting my money. I'm utilising it to do what I want to do, what I like doing. If I don't want to get stuck in a nine to five job which seems monotonous to me, that's my choice, and I cannot possibly be doing nothing if I'm exercising my choice. Thirdly, I'm a decent chef, a language teacher, a dancer, and a singer because I travel and learn a variety of things," he answered.

"You don't want to settle down because maybe you are scared…," she said.

"Scared of?" he asked.

"Scared of maybe responsibilities, conforming to codes of conduct, or maybe you are selfish, maybe you just want to have fun with no work," she answered.

"I am rather courageous. You know why? Because I'm living the life I want to live. And trust me, that is a really courageous task," he answered.

"But people can't always do what they like. I understand that you like visiting new places. Everybody does that. But after doing that, they come back to their normal routine. They have things to do, a life to live," she said.

"People visit places as a part of their lives. It is not their life," she added when he did not say anything.

"So according to you, living a life is synonymous with being stationary and confined to a place? If I don't have a fixed home and a fixed profession, I'm wasting my chance to 'live a life'?" he asked back, putting the last three words in quotes.

"Okay. You keep travelling. Then what? You won't have a family? Or will your family keep moving with you? Do you have any money saved in case of any misfortune? No, right? Aditya! Travelling is a hobby. Not a profession. You'll have to get settled someday," she continued.

"After people complete their studies and before they get married, what do they do? They pursue their hobby and make their careers. Right? So if I'm travelling all this while, I'm simply pursuing my hobby and trying out available career options like being a chef, a dancer, a singer and people pay me for that, trust me," he replied.

"Why is the word 'settled' synonymous with fixedness? Doesn't settling down signify that you are content with your life? I'm content with my life at this point, and therefore, I feel settled. If my 'settled' is your 'unsettled', that's not my problem," he added.

"You are not getting me." She sighed again.

She wanted to leave but he continued, "I'll start a family once I meet someone with whom I would want to spend the rest of my life and I don't know how or when that would happen or what would I do then. I call myself a traveller right now because that's what I've been doing since eight years now and I don't want to quit it anytime soon. Maybe I'll die with it, and maybe I won't."

She remained silent.

"Anyway, could you please tell me about some points of interest here? The taxi driver did tell me about some places, but a second opinion would be great," he said.

She told him about the Tiger Hill, the Cactus Nursery, Rock Garden, Buddhist Tibetan Monastery, Botanical Gardens and nearby places like Kalimpong, Sikkim, Siliguri.

He thanked her and made up his mind to visit the Tiger Hill, early in the morning.

This conversation left a grave impact on the minds of both Aditya and Zinnia. They both couldn't sleep that night and thought about the conversation over and over for days.

After having dinner, Aditya went to his room and tried to sleep. But he couldn't. Zinnia's words kept echoing in his head. He knew that the world thought just like her and he would never be 'settled' in the traditional sense, if he was a traveller. He liked to travel. If someone can be a doctor if he likes it or a teacher or an actor or a psychiatrist or anyone with a roof over his head which is secure, with a fixed income and food security, it's alright. But if he wants to be a traveller, it's not, because there's no security. Youth is the best phase to travel and he was young. He didn't want to waste his energy and vigour doing something he wasn't interested in.

These thoughts kept recurring in his head and to distract himself, he went towards the drawer and took out his wooden box of mementos which he had collected while travelling to different places. He looked at the wooden ship from Kerala, sea shells from Goa, tea leaves from Assam, and then his eyes stopped at the silver Buddha which he had received as a gift from a girl in Chandigarh.

Her name was Sara. Aditya was a paying guest at her house where she lived with her mother and father. She had become good friends with Aditya during his stay at the house. She sang really well, so one day her mother urged her to participate in a singing competition that was two months away. But she refused and became red with fury whenever her mother discussed the matter. She would leave the dining table, the room, the kitchen and sometimes the house, whenever her mother would talk about it. Her mother couldn't figure out what the problem was since she was an excellent singer and wouldn't mind taking it up as a profession. Concerned about her daughter's erratic behaviour, she went to Aditya as she knew that they bonded well, and told him about her problem. Aditya promised to do something about it.

"Hey Sara!" Aditya greeted her as she sat in the garden.

"Hey! What's up?" she replied.

"Nothing much. Visited the Hand monument today. You tell? What did you do?" he asked.

"Nothing," she answered, lowering her face.

"Hey, I have heard about some singing competition. Are you taking part in it?" He came to the point.

"No," she answered.

"Why?" he asked back.

"Don't have time," she began to get up.

"Hey wait!" He pulled her back.

"I'm sure you can manage. Plus, this is a rare opportunity. Your career will hit new milestones if you win this, and you have that potential. You have such a beautiful voice. Try singing here and you'll attract a huge audience," he tried to convince her.

"I know but…," she hesitated.

"What happened, Sara? What's troubling you?" he asked.

She looked down.

"We're friends right? Come on, tell me!" he asked again.

"Aditya! Look at me! Do I look like a singer? I am fat and ugly. My hairstyle is shabby. I don't have pretty features. Everybody will make fun of me! I don't want them to say that I sing like a nightingale and look like a crow." She gave in.

"Sara, shut up! Firstly, you don't have to look like a singer. You've to sound like one. Secondly, you are not ugly. If you're not comfortable with how you look, join a gym, follow a balanced diet and you'll no longer be fat. Go to the parlour; get a haircut which suits you and your hair will be fine. And your features are fine. You're not ugly, Sara! You're beautiful," he consoled her.

"Beautiful, eh?" She made fun of him.

"Tell me, if the words you spoke appeared on your face, will you be beautiful?" he asked her.

She kept looking at him and blinked.

"Yes, you'll be the prettiest girl on earth then! Sara, your problems are not something you can't change and you know that. You are just not accepting it. You are afraid of doing anything because you fear the outcome. Why do you fear it? Are you afraid about what will happen if you fail? Because you've got an excuse now, but you won't have it then, right? No competition, no losing," he said.

She nodded.

"I don't have the courage to face the world," she said.

"Do you have the courage to face the fact that you're not courageous?" he asked back.

She remained silent.

"Sara! Go for it. You've got two months. Lose weight, practice singing in these two months. If you win it, your career gets a boost. If you don't, you'll be saved from the embarrassment and guilt of not giving it a shot. You have to do it for yourself otherwise you'll lose all respect for yourself in your own eyes a few months down the line. I know you, Sara. Trust me, you'll win it and be successful thereafter. I've heard you sing. I have full faith in you. You'll beat them all. You know me Sara and you know I wouldn't say all this just to please you. You have to try." He urged her.

She smiled and nodded.

For two months, Sara became his top-most priority. He saw to it that she followed her schedule, diet charts, gym routines, practice sessions, college, everything, without getting too exhausted. He took care of her health and kept motivating her. Sara lost nine kgs in two months and got rid of her inferiority complex. Her skin improved with the diet and it started glowing. He became the man behind her success, and led her to win that trophy.

He didn't leave her at just that. He prolonged his stay in Chandigarh and stood by her side till she bagged a Punjabi Album, lost twenty kgs more and gained enough confidence to handle any situation. He stayed for nine months in Chandigarh and in these months, he changed and made a life.

Sara didn't want him to go, but he had to. He had to go for his happiness. His happiness was in exploring and travelling. And so he continued with his next journey.

Even after two years, he remembered everything like it had happened yesterday. He could visualise how he and Sara had hugged each other, crying sadly, breaking apart when he was leaving. He could bring forth from the share of his memory how Sara tried to stop him from going, how resistant she was to his decision of leaving, and how he had promised her that she would find him within herself, in her memories, whenever she would need him.

He looked at the shining silver Buddha in his hand, still fresh after two years. He took a deep breath and closed the box. He took the Buddha with him to bed and with it on his side, he fell asleep.

He had collected a zillion memories while he travelled. Some were profound, some vague, some still brought tears, some made him feel nothing, but out of all the memories that he wreathed, Sara's stood apart.

Endearment

Aditya woke up early the next morning as he had to witness sunrise at the Tiger Hill. He left the house while it was still dark and took a taxi to the Tiger Hill.

He reached the spot on time and sat down at a place from where the best view could be seen. The dark blue and purple of the twilight sky were slowly overthrown by the bright streaks of red, yellow, pink and orange. Resembling a prism, the sky witnessed all the colours blended perfectly into each other. The first orange hued rays of sunrise kissed the sky and the soft rays brought warmth to a new day.

Aditya marvelled at the glistening sun and the breathtaking display of radiant colours.

He was so enamoured by the beautiful natural phenomenon he had just witnessed that he decided to sit there the whole day.

"I wouldn't leave without witnessing the sunset," he told the driver.

He waited the entire day for the sunset to occur. Soon, his wish was fulfilled.

He watched the sunset with an unwavering gaze, as a fiery red orb of light slowly sank beneath the horizon. The sky appeared first orange, then red and then dark blue. Slowly, the sky turned into a clear purple-tinged grey and the threads of light lingering in the sky melted away, giving way to darkness.

"I would have regretted it all my life, if I hadn't waited for the sunset," he told the driver as they headed back.

"I forgot everything for a while, who I was, where did I come from, why I am here, everything. It was just the universe and me. Such a beautiful phenomenon. Amazing!" he added.

"Yes, sir. Indeed." the driver replied.

Even when he came inside the house, he was not able to get the natural phenomena out of his mind and he was more cheerful than usual. He took out his guitar from the almirah and went out to the Mall Road. It was crowded as usual. At night, the lights looked more beautiful and not being able to resist while the soft cold breeze teased his cheeks, he sat down at a corner and started singing while playing the guitar. Everybody could feel the joy in his voice and those who heard him forgot all their worries and sat down with him. He attracted a large audience. Those who passed by stopped to hear him and couldn't resist themselves from singing a line or two with him or humming to his tune.

He sang in Hindi, English, Korean and French. All blended up, mixed together, portraying secularity in music and people around joined him.

A restaurant owner heard him and offered him to sing in his restaurant on the coming weekend. The crowd urged him to say 'yes' and he couldn't refuse. Ecstatic, he came back to his room and had dinner. All the pending dues of the previous night when he couldn't sleep properly were paid that night and he enjoyed a sound sleep.

When Aditya woke up the next morning, he saw Sid sitting beside him, looking at his face.

"What's up, lad? What are you doing here?" he asked, stretching himself and getting up.

"Nothing. I was getting bored, so I came to talk to you, but you were sleeping. Then I thought I should draw something on your face, but then remembered that you are our guest. So I just sat here, thinking what to do with you." Sid replied.

Aditya laughed and fell in love with his innocence.

"Who taught you Hindi?" he asked.

"They teach us Hindi in school. Though I am not fluent, I've started getting the hang of it." the boy replied.

"Okay! So why didn't you go to school today?" Aditya asked, picking Sid up to make him sit on his lap.

"We have an off today. Some festival." he replied.

"Hmm…I see," Aditya kissed him on his cheeks and continued to ask, "How old are you?"

"Ten, you?" the kid asked back.

Aditya laughed and asked "Me?" in a childish manner.

Sid nodded.

"Well, I am just thirty-one," he replied.

"What do you do?" the boy asked.

"I travel to different places." Aditya replied.

"What all places have you been to?" Sid asked.

"Umm… Many… Wait, I'll show you something."

Aditya picked up the wooden box and opened it for Sid.

"All these things are from the places I have visited," he said.

Sid was amazed at the collection and picked up a nicely decorated small box made of jute with ribbons around it.

"This is so beautiful!" he exclaimed.

"This is from Lansdowne," Aditya said.

"Lans…," Sid tried to pronounce the name of the place.

"Downe… Lans… Downe…," Aditya helped him.

"And this?" Sid asked while smelling an aroma candle.

"Nainital. Doesn't it smell nice," Aditya asked.

"Yes. I love it. What is it?" the boy asked.

"It's a candle which smells nice." Aditya replied.

Sid checked out other things and asked Aditya if he would take him to all these places.

"If only your elder sister allows!" Aditya answered.

They both giggled.

"You know, there's a big garden on my way back home from school. I want to go there and play but Zinnia is always busy." Sid said.

"I'll accompany you someday, but don't go alone." Aditya said.

"Sid! Sid! Where are you?" Zinnia came inside Aditya's room, searching for Sid.

"Sid! This is not a good thing. You can't disturb uncle early in the morning," she said coming towards Sid.

Sid grabbed her hand and made her sit on the bed.

"Look at these things, Zinnia! How lovely they are! Aditya uncle got them from the places he travelled to. See!" said the young boy, in an excited voice.

He made her see a wooden tree collectible from Nainital, aroma candles, sea shells and the silver Buddha. Zinnia liked the things very much and was ecstatic to touch the sea shells. She looked at the things with a twinkle in her eyes, just like a child. Suddenly, she remembered something and sadness started to creep in onto her face.

"Come Sid! Let uncle freshen up now!" she put the box on the bed and held Sid's hand.

"Okay uncle. Bye!" The young boy waved at Aditya.

"Bye Sid!" Aditya waved back.

"Listen, Zinnia!" he called her from behind.

She stopped and turned around.

"I'll have breakfast here today. I hope that's fine," he asked.

"Yes, I'll give it in your room," she answered.

"Thanks!" Aditya said.

Aditya stayed at home to play with Sid the entire day. He taught him different games which he had learnt from kids at various places. Sid was a fast learner. He got the hang of almost all of them.

Mrs. Anita was not there in the house for the entire day. In her absence, Zinnia took care of everything. Zinnia was the caretaker of the house – she prepared meals, cleaned the house, took care of Sid and did everything Mrs. Anita asked her to do. In the evening, Aditya was stepping out of the house to get fresh air, when he saw Zinnia sitting at the entrance, looking at the Travel section of a magazine. Her eyes were fixated upon an exotic setting with dark surroundings lit up by lanterns where a boat stood in a small pond with vegetation all around.

"You like it?" Aditya asked, bending down to sit beside her.

She quickly closed the magazine and kept it away.

"What happened? Why did you put it away?" Aditya asked.

"I didn't find it interesting enough," she replied.

"But I saw you looking at it," he said.

"I look at a lot of things, but that doesn't mean I like all of them. I am not in love with the idea of places and settings like you," she said this while getting up.

Aditya couldn't understand her behaviour, but he knew that she was hiding something. He picked up the magazine and put it on the table inside the house. Afterwards, he went for a walk and sang his heart out again at the Mall Road.

Three days passed.

Aditya had gone to visit the Buddha Temple when he came back around 3:00 p.m. and saw Zinnia moving around in the house. She looked extremely worried.

"Hey, what happened? You look worried?" Aditya asked.

"Sid…I can't find him," Zinnia started crying.

"Zinnia, relax! Tell me what happened. I'll help you. Tell me." He tried to calm her down.

"I went to Sid's school to pick him up. But he wasn't there. I asked the guard. He said he was there a few moments ago. He just disappeared. I checked inside the school, every nook and corner, but he wasn't there. I checked in the nearby streets. I asked his friends, their parents, neighbours. I checked at the Mall Road. He is nowhere! I don't know where he's gone. If mother comes back and she doesn't find him inside the house, she'll get really upset. She'll never forgive me. Sid is my responsibility," she explained.

"Please…Please do something. Please get him back. Please…," she grabbed Aditya's hands and begged him to get Sid back.

"Zinnia, don't worry. I'll do something. I'm here. I'll get him back." He consoled her, putting his hand on her face and back onto her hand.

Aditya went outside the house, towards the school, thinking where he could go.

He asked people on the way about Sid. He looked at every corner of the road taking him towards the school. After walking for some distance, he saw a garden and remembered Sid's words about how he wanted to visit this garden near his school. He went inside the garden, asking the people if they had seen a small boy of around ten, checking behind every tree, every bench, every swing, when his eyes fell on a nearby tree with a honeycomb on one of its branches.

"Sid!" He shouted.

Sid rushed towards him and hugged hm. He picked him up, hugged him even tighter, kissed his forehead and cheeks and said, "What are you doing here, alone? I told you not to come here alone. Why did you do this?" He scolded Sid.

"I am sorry. I was really afraid. I couldn't find the way to go outside the garden. This garden is so big. I was lost." Sid hugged Aditya and rested his chin on Aditya's left shoulder.

"Sid, I didn't expect this from you. You should have thought about Zinnia before doing this. Do you even know how worried she is? I told you I'll accompany you. I told you not to go alone. You didn't listen to me. Aren't we friends? Shouldn't you listen to your friend?" Aditya said.

"Sorry. I'll apologize to Zinnia too. I'll listen to you. You are my best friend. Please take me home." The young boy apologized.

They came back home. Aditya told Zinnia everything.

"I am sorry, Sid! I didn't know you wanted to go to the garden so badly. I had a lot of work at home since a couple of days and there was so much stitching work pending! I am sorry. Please don't do this again. Don't punish me like this." Zinnia started crying.

"Hey, hey, hey... Zinnia! Zinnia, it's okay! Sid understands. Zinnia... look at me... you are a great sister. Sid loves you. It's alright." Aditya consoled her.

Sid kissed her and promised to never repeat it ever again. He hugged Aditya and Zinnia together, and in that moment, they looked like family.

Sid convinced Zinnia to go to the restaurant where Aditya would be singing on Saturday. Zinnia was reluctant to go, but couldn't refuse Sid. She wasn't still over Sid's act. Meanwhile, Aditya had become known to many people around. He loved meeting people. When he walked on the road, he made sure he did something good for people who looked worried. He greeted old people and talked to them, which made them feel important, since not many people had the time to do that. If he saw a hungry dog, he would buy him food. He would greet shopkeepers in an affectionate manner. He spread happiness wherever he went. His desire to really understand people and not just converse with them had a positive impact on him and people's lives and it was this quality for which he was admired the most. Neither did anyone have the time to do what he was doing, nor the willingness. His good deeds won many hearts.

He delivered an incredible performance on Saturday. Zinnia had come along with Sid and Rita, one of her few friends. As soon as Aditya started singing, the crowd in the restaurant started swinging to his beats. He sang from the heart. He sang for himself. His voice reminded some of their lost loves, some of a brighter future, some of their beautiful present and some of those moments which were enough to live a lifetime. His words touched the core. Rita went crazy for him after the performance. Many people came up to him to ask about him and his talent. That by itself was his achievement. He was immediately booked for the month to sing on Saturdays at the restaurant and was paid his due. Zinnia congratulated him for a successful event and together with Sid, they went back home.

"How did it go?" Mrs. Anita asked when they came home.

"Mom, it was amazing. He is a star!" Sid shouted. The lady smiled and asked Aditya to have dinner with them. Aditya was flattered and accepted the offer.

For the entire night, Zinnia couldn't get Aditya's voice out of her head. She tried to sleep, but his voice echoed in her ears. She kept changing sides on her bed. Tired of doing that, she got up to drink water from the kitchen when she passed by Aditya's room and saw the lights turned on. She quickly drank water and went back to her room.

Concern

The following day was a Sunday. The family went to the local zoo for recreation, except Zinnia. Aditya had planned to visit Kalimpong but dropped the idea as he woke up late in the morning, almost at noon.

He came out of his room after freshening up to eat something from a nearby restaurant. He saw Zinnia cleaning the house.

"Good afternoon!" he greeted her.

She didn't reply.

On coming closer, he realised that she was about to faint. He held her. Zinnia regained her balance.

"Are you alright?" he asked her.

"I don't know what's happening. I am feeling weak," she replied.

He touched her forehead and cheeks with the back of his hand.

"You have fever, Zinnia. Come, drop this broom!" he said.

"No, I have to clean the house," she answered in a low voice.

"It's not imperative to clean the house every day. You can skip it once in a while. Come now," he said.

"No...," she replied.

He snatched the broom from her hand, held her arm and took her to her room.

"Lie down! I'll give you the medicines and then you'll sleep," he said in a commanding tone.

"I can't sleep. I have to prepare a meal for tonight's dinner. Mom's friends are coming to our house for dinner," she replied in a nimble voice.

"You tell your mom that you were unwell. She can order something from outside," he said.

"No, I've promised her. I can't do that. I'll have to get up otherwise I'll get late in preparing the meal," she replied, trying to get up.

"No, you can't get up. Lie down!" he ordered.

As an afterthought, Aditya looked at Zinnia and said, "Can I help you? I know how to cook. I've worked as a chef in resorts before. You tell me what to prepare and I'll do it."

"No, my mom will know. She knows the taste," she replied, sounding worried.

"She is your mom, Zinnia! She'll understand that her daughter wasn't well." He tried to convince her.

"But...," she couldn't speak further.

"First tell me, do you keep some medicines in your house?" he asked.

"Yes."

"Where are they?" he asked.

"There, in that drawer on the table beside the cupboard."

He took out the medicine from the drawer and poured water from the jug on the side table into the glass.

"You had your breakfast?" he asked.

"Yes," she answered.

"Then you're good to go. Here, take it!" he said.

She took the medicine and he continued, "Trust me. I won't let you down in front of everyone. I am a decent cook. Please trust me this time. I'll take the blame on myself if I don't live up to their expectations or yours. I'll tell everyone that I forced you to let me cook. Now please tell me what to make."

Zinnia nodded.

"Noodles, chicken momos, chilli sauce and chicken sandwiches," she answered.

"Great! I'll need your help in momos. I'll prepare the rest and one dessert too. Okay?" he replied.

She nodded again.

"So, you sleep now. I'll prepare the meal. When you wake up, you can help me with momos or else I'll wake you up two hours before dinner time. Okay?" he asked.

"Yes… They said they'll come at 7:00p.m., but they can come early as well. They have gone to the Zoo together," she replied.

"Great! So you sleep now," he said.

Everything was ready when Zinnia woke up at 4:30 p.m., except the dessert. Aditya was making a chocolate pudding when he saw Zinnia enter the kitchen.

"How are you feeling? Better?" he asked.

"Yes…," she replied.

"I was feeling hungry so I ate the chapatis that you had kept. I'll have my dinner outside then. Now, taste this," he said, putting the fork with noodles in her mouth.

"They taste good. I thought you were joking about having worked as a chef," she said.

"No, I really have," he said laughing.

She tasted everything he had prepared and she loved it.

They made momos together and soon the pudding was ready.

At sharp 7:00p.m., everyone was seated at the dining table. Zinnia served the guests. Everyone praised Zinnia for the food before leaving. By then, Aditya had come back after having his dinner. He had brought fresh juice for Zinnia and kept it in the kitchen.

"I haven't made the food today. Aditya did," she told everyone.

She called Aditya and introduced him to everyone.

"Boy, you cook really well," said a lady.

"Thank you, ma'am. Actually Zinnia wasn't well today. I saw that she was about to faint. So I just helped her. Besides, I love cooking," he said.

"Zinnia, what happened? How are you now?" Mrs. Anita asked.

"I'm fine now. Just a little fever. I'll be okay," she replied.

The guests took leave.

"I've got fresh juice for you. Have your dinner and drink it. You'll feel much better, and then take your medicine on time before sleeping." Aditya said to Zinnia before going to his room.

Zinnia did as instructed.

Aditya came out of his room at night to check if Zinnia was okay and if she had taken the juice. She was sleeping. He was relieved to see that she had done everything as he had said. Afterwards, he also went to sleep.

The following day, the first thing he did after waking up was to search for Zinnia in the house. He found her in the gallery.

"How are you feeling now? Do you still have fever?" he asked.

"I'm good now," she answered.

"So the fever must be due to exhaustion. You have made yourself weak. You keep roaming around all day due to household chores and other tasks. You need to rest a bit," he said.

"Hmm... I couldn't thank you for yesterday. Thanks a lot for the food. You've saved me for the second time," she said, smiling. She had smiled for the first time while talking to him in all this time!

"I didn't help you. I love cooking and hadn't done that for a while. I was just looking for a chance to cook and you gave that to me. So, thanks to you," he replied, smiling back.

"You're so humble," she said.

"Please don't exhaust yourself today. Please take rest, okay?" he said.

She nodded. She smiled again.

"By the way, you look prettier when you smile." He complimented her.

She blushed.

He went inside the room to get dressed for the day.

After getting dressed, he thought that he should stay at home for the day so that he could help Zinnia if she needed something or felt unwell. But after knowing that Mrs. Anita was to be at home for the entire day, he thought that Zinnia had her mother to take care of her and so he went out. He visited a cactus nursery that day. He didn't plan an elaborate sightseeing trip, so he came back early in the evening.

He had skipped his lunch because he didn't feel like eating. He couldn't enjoy being outside and exploring different varieties of cactus in the nursery, while his mind was somewhere else. He was thinking of Zinnia and if she was well. He was concerned about her. For the first time after being a traveller, he regretted not carrying a mobile phone. He wasn't a gadget person. Besides, he didn't feel the need for it.

After getting back, he went straight towards the kitchen. He pretended that he was feeling thirsty while all he wanted was a glimpse of Zinnia to know that she was alright. Zinnia was working in the kitchen. The sight of her being well and safe gave him immense satisfaction. After freshening up, he walked towards the door of his room to ask Zinnia for food, but he stood at his place behind the door when he heard Mrs. Anita scolding Zinnia

"Why have you made the dal so spicy? Where were you lost while cooking?" she shouted furiously at Zinnia.

"But mother, I put the same amount which I put every day. I tasted it after cooking. It seemed fine to me," she replied in a low voice, almost on the verge of breaking down.

"So, I'm lying? If I'm saying it doesn't seem fine to me, it isn't! Alright? How dare you answer me back?" She shouted again.

"Oh! I got it. The behaviour is because of what happened yesterday, right? That man helped you yesterday and sympathised with you, so you have started feeling like a princess now, isn't it?" She continued.

"No mother. I'm sorry. I'll make something again. Please forgive me." Zinnia apologised.

"Why? Do you get all these things for free? You want to increase our expenses? Now princess Zinnia will waste things because she was lost in her own world of dreams while cooking!" She taunted her.

Zinnia started crying and ran to her room. She locked it from inside.

Aditya felt really bad. He wanted to intervene, but couldn't. It was their family matter and after all, Mrs. Anita was Zinnia's mother. He chose to keep quiet and went inside to lie down on his bed.

After a few minutes, Sid came back to the house with his father. He had gone to the Mall Road to get a new toy.

"Has uncle come?" he asked his mother.

"Yes, he's in his room," his mother replied.

He knocked the door and Aditya allowed him to come in.

"Hello uncle!" he said cheerfully.

"Hello! How are you? How was your day at school?" Aditya replied.

"I'm great. My day was really good. How was yours? Where did you go?" asked the young boy.

"I went to a cactus nursery. It was lovely," he replied.

"Uncle, I wanted to ask for a favour," he said.

"Yes, what happened?" Aditya replied in a low voice.

He was really upset about what he had just witnessed.

"I told my friends about those things in your box which you had collected. They want to see your collection too. So can you bring them to my school tomorrow when it gets over or I can bring my friends to the house and you allow them inside your room," requested Sid.

Aditya smiled.

"Sure," he replied.

"Thank you uncle!" Sid thanked him excitedly.

Sid went out of the room happily.

Aditya lied down again. Mrs. Anita's words kept echoing in his ears and Zinnia's face in his mind. He couldn't understand why Mrs. Anita reacted like that to a matter as small as that. He kept looking for reasons that would explain her reaction, but he couldn't think of any, which could justify what she had said to the poor girl. Zinnia was the meekest person in front of her mother. He hadn't seen a child so obedient and scared of her mother's wrath. Maybe she had some health concerns or maybe she had a bad day, maybe the food was very spicy and that irritated her, maybe she was concerned about Sid or her husband, Mr. Hudson, eating it. There could be plausible reasons to make her angry but none to justify her words.

The clock had struck 9:00 p.m. Aditya hadn't asked for dinner nor had he gone out. Zinnia came to his room to ask if he would like to have his dinner, since he hadn't eaten in the house today. He was in no mood to have food but replied in the affirmative.

When the food was served to him, the first thing he did was taste the dal. It seemed perfect to him. It wasn't spicy at all. Zinnia was pouring water in his jug at that time.

He wanted to ask why her mother was so angry at her because there was absolutely nothing wrong with the dal. He couldn't, though. She went out of the room and he couldn't say a word. He finished eating and went to the kitchen to keep the dirty plate in the sink. He found Sid standing near the refrigerator. He bent down and asked Sid if the dal was spicy when he ate it.

Sid replied in the negative. He asked him not to mention it to anyone that he had asked about it. Sid agreed.

Sid's answer confused Aditya even more. He still couldn't dare ask Zinnia as he had no right to interfere in their family matters. The best reason he could give to himself was that Zinnia added some other ingredients later to make the dal taste less spicy and conducive to be consumed.

Before sleeping, Aditya thought about what Sid had told him. He came up with an idea. He thought that there might be other children and adults who would want to see his collection once they knew about it, so for the benefit of everyone, he decided to host an exhibition of his collection for the students at Sid's school after taking the permission from the concerned authorities and for the people at large in a garden. Both would be free of cost.

The next day, he went to Sid's school and sought the permission from the principal, who readily agreed. He was lucky in this regard as the very next day the school was to have some of its cultural events. Without hesitating for a second, he asked the principal to arrange for a canopy for the following day where he would be displaying his collection and asked for further details. Aditya had to prepare a lot of stuff for the exhibition, so he quickly went back to the house after the meeting got over.

Aditya asked Zinnia for pieces of white paper when he got back home. Zinnia gave them to him. After that, he started writing the names of the places from where the mementos were, in bold letters. He kept the box in a bag, thought of inspiring stories which he could tell the children of the places he visited, thought of the placement of different items on the table and went to the market to buy a packet of candies which he could give to the children. He put the papers in thick plastic sheets which Zinnia arranged for him. He told Sid about his plan when Sid came back home in the evening after playing with his friends.

The following day, he reached school on time at 11:00 a.m. He displayed his items on the table inside the canopy. He made compartments of different places and placed the plastic sheets on the items of each place. The students came to see his exhibition with their teachers as per their internal schedule. One of the students picked up the silver Buddha to take it home. His teacher saw him and asked him to keep it back. Aditya was busy distributing candies at that time. The students touched the things, played with them and loved them. They behaved well as there were a lot of teachers around to keep an eye on them.

Sid told everyone proudly that Aditya was his friend and lived in his house. His teachers shook hands with Aditya and so did his friends. The exhibition was successful. Aditya told inspiring stories like Sara's to the children. He talked about his adventures and exotic experiences. The teachers loved listening to his tales. He had become a hero that day. Aditya was later invited for lunch with the principal.

Sid told Zinnia about the day. Zinnia then figured out why Aditya was asking for plastic sheets and white paper, which she had found weird the previous day.

After getting great response from school, Aditya was ecstatic about his next exhibition which he planned to conduct on Sunday. He talked to local association members of a popular garden and the day was finalised.

He spread the word by asking the people he knew to come to the exhibition and inform others. He took some sheets from Zinnia and wrote on them, "TRAVEL EXHIBITION – A SNAPSHOT OF ADITYA'S TRAVEL DIARIES," "FREE OF

COST", with the date and venue. He pasted the sheets on places which witness high footfall.

In all this, he didn't realise when the week came to an end. It was Saturday when he decided to stay at home and prepare for his show at night. He sat on the stairs in front of the house door and looked at people passing by. He found the gallery quite picturesque and acknowledged Zinnia's efforts in keeping the plants so healthy, in his mind. The plants and the flowers were blooming. The boundaries of the gallery were well marked by different plants. The flowers of vibrant colours beautified the place. There was nobody in the house except Zinnia. On seeing Aditya sitting outside, she came and sat beside him. She didn't ignore him anymore.

"Sid told me about your exhibition at school. You had another successful event," she said smiling.

Aditya smiled back and thanked her.

"So, how is it going? Do you still feel weak at times?" he asked.

"No, I take adequate rest now," she replied.

"You've kept the plants really well. Your efforts have paid off." He complimented her. She smiled.

A lady passed by, hurriedly. She was talking on phone saying she will be right there at the hospital. Aditya and Zinnia heard that.

"So a mobile phone is useful too. It helps you when you're in need. Why don't you keep one? What if you're in need of help someday? A mobile phone can come in handy," Aditya asked Zinnia.

"I hardly go out of the house. I don't think I need one," she answered.

Before he could say something, she asked him the same.

"I don't feel the need. Maybe I would feel it when I get stuck in a crisis," he said, smiling.

"Don't you have people you would stay in contact with? You're away from your home. How does your family contact you?" she asked.

"I don't have parents. They passed away in an accident when I was still a child. My paternal grandparents were with them. They were going for some work. They died too," he said.

His eyes had started to water.

"Oh, I am so sorry. So whom did you live with all this while, if I may ask?" She continued.

"My maternal grandparents. My mother was their only child. They died as they were not well. Old age hit them. First my grandmother died, then my grandfather. I was the only child of my parents. I have no siblings. Same was with my father. When my grandfather died, I decided to become a traveller." He narrated his story.

A drop of tear rolled down his cheek.

"So I've nobody to call," he said trying to veil his pain behind a smile after wiping his tears.

"I feel bad for you…," Zinnia said apologetically.

"Don't you make friends at the places you visit?" she asked.

"I do, but who has the time to stay in touch. I don't stay at one place. Nobody stays in touch after their friends leave town. They get busy with their lives. What remains is only memories," he answered.

"True," she said.

"So, what's your story?" he asked her.

She didn't say anything.

"How old are you?" he asked.

"Twenty-one," she answered.

"You completed your schooling?" he asked.

"Yes. I didn't attend college. After school, I started taking care of the house and Sid. I do embroidery and sewing work. People give me orders. I like it," she replied.

"Hmm… so you've been living here since childhood?" he asked.

She nodded.

"So tell me about your childhood, your dreams, your family, your memories…," he said.

Before she could share anything, they saw Rita coming towards them.

"I saw Mrs. Anita going towards the market so I came to give you company, thinking you might be alone," said Rita to Zinnia. She smiled.

Rita greeted Aditya. Aditya greeted back.

"I didn't get a chance to fully appreciate your performance that day. You sang really well." She complimented Aditya.

"Thank you," Aditya replied.

"I have a show today also, and for all Saturdays of this month. Same time, same place. Do come," he added.

"Surely. We'll come," she said looking at Zinnia.

"I'm not sure," Zinnia replied.

"I'll tell Sid and he'll make sure that you come."

All three of them laughed.

"So ladies, I'll leave you alone to talk your hearts out! See you," said Aditya, getting up.

"No, no. Sit! Let's chat!" said Rita, making him sit.

"I have heard your stories. People recognise you here," she continued.

They talked for hours about their lives, people, places and things. Rita told them about Samara, a young girl of fourteen, who fell on a downhill road and hurt her legs so bad that she was on a wheelchair now. Her family decided to leave the area as it was difficult to take Samara everywhere on the wheelchair due to the mountains. They would shift to a plain area in a couple of days. Aditya felt bad for the girl and asked Rita if she could introduce him to her.

"I'll talk to the family tomorrow and let you know," she answered.

Before leaving, Rita asked if they could go somewhere to hang out and have fun. They would also get to know each other better then.

"It's been ages since I have gone out with friends. Come on guys! Me, Aditya and you, Zinnia. It'll be fun. We can take Sid along if aunty agrees," she said.

Zinnia was hesitant. She knew that Rita liked Aditya and was looking for a chance to know him better.

"You two can go. I have a lot of work these days." Zinnia replied.

"Please, Zinnia! Please, please, please!" Rita requested.

Zinnia couldn't refuse. Although she knew that Mrs. Anita wouldn't allow her and would get mad at her, she still promised Rita that she would ask her.

"Thank you...," Rita hugged her, and left.

When Mrs. Anita came home late in the afternoon, Zinnia asked her if she could go with Rita and Aditya and also take Sid along.

"How dare you even ask me this? Have you lost your mind?" She scolded Zinnia.

By then, Aditya had come back after having his lunch. He overheard the conversation, standing outside the main door.

"And how did you even think that I'll send Sid along with you? You are so careless! I'll never even dream of doing that. You're not going anywhere either. You get it? We haven't raised you for your outings. Who will do the house work? And whose plan was this? How dare does that girl come to our house? Or did you go outside? Tell me? And what's Aditya to do with all this? What's going on Zinnia?" She kept shouting and throwing a zillion questions at Zinnia.

"Listen to me Zinnia. It's my house. You'll follow my rules. Never ask me for such stupid things again." She shouted again.

"And don't tell Rita or Aditya that I refused. Tell them you have work or you don't want to go or whatever, but don't you dare mention my name. Now go, make tea for me. You have given me a headache!" She went on and on.

Zinnia listened quietly with her face hanging low. She had expected this. But it was better to ask than break Rita's heart by not trying.

She went inside the kitchen and sobbed.

Aditya was infuriated at Mrs. Anita. He wanted to go inside and put some sense into her mind, but he controlled himself. He didn't even want to see her face, so he went to his room without even looking at her. He hated her at that moment. He had lost all respect for the lady. But he knew one thing. If something like that were to happen again, he would definitely show Mrs. Anita the mirror so as to how that lady ought to thank Zinnia for what she did for the house rather than shout at her without any point using such harsh words which were absolutely uncalled for.

Aditya was in a spoilt mood. He didn't feel like singing at all. But after seeing Zinnia with Rita and Sid at the show, his face lightened up. As he saw her smile, he started singing from the heart. He picked up with his music and soon after a few songs, his show became a success like the previous one. Zinnia's smile was his muse this time.

After the show got over, Aditya invited Rita to his exhibition the next day and apologised for forgetting to do that in the morning itself. All of them went home happily after that.

The next day, Aditya reached the venue hours before the exhibition was to start. On reaching the garden, he found an old woman crying while sitting on one of the benches. He went to sit beside her. He kept his things aside and started talking to her.

"Hello!" he greeted her.

She didn't reply.

"Why are you crying?" he asked.

"Who are you? And what do you want from me?" she asked rudely.

"Amma… I'm like your son. What happened? Tell me!" He showed his concern.

"Why should I tell you anything? You're a stranger," she replied.

"I have an exhibition here today. Many people who know me would be coming here today. I have no bad intentions. If you don't want to tell me your problem, then don't. But I request you to please listen to me for some time. Can you do that?" he said.

She didn't say anything but kept sitting on the bench. He took it as an indication to continue.

"You know…once my grandfather had a fight with my grandmother, he spoke some really harsh words. She felt unwanted and left the house without telling him. I was a kid then. I urged my grandfather to get her back. My grandfather called everyone he knew, but couldn't gather any information. We had to live for two days without her. Then she couldn't resist herself and came to meet me in school. I told her how pathetic my grandfather had been feeling without her. I made her tell me where she was staying. I came back home and made my grandfather realise his love for her and his mistake. Then we went to get her back.

"After that my grandfather never talked to her badly. We lived like a happy family. But when I grew up, I got busy with my studies and other things, friends… I couldn't live up to her expectations regarding how much time should I spend with her. My grandfather was busy earning. She started feeling neglected, and I sensed that. I loved her, but I had to give time to other things too. I couldn't neglect them either. I was growing up. So I asked her to keep herself busy with the things she liked. I asked her to work for a charitable institution or a welfare association or go for a walk every day. She followed that. Soon, she began to feel healthy as she didn't take unnecessary stress and had people to talk to. Being socially active made her feel good about herself, passing time became easier and she contributed something good to society."

The old woman smiled. He had touched the right nerve.

"Amma, I understand your loneliness. But trust me, your children love you, but they have a really hectic life. They are struggling every day. Life has become really fast. They need to run, fall and then run again. Your life is in your hands. Any empty mind is a devil's home."

She patted him on his head and thanked him.

He had made somebody smile again. He felt happy. He took her blessings and went to prepare for the exhibition.

He set the things the way he had done at school. At the scheduled time, people started coming in. He wished for Zinnia to come. People were really interested in his stories and collections. The event entertained an audience of hundred people in just an hour. Aditya got really busy amidst entertaining the crowd.

A young boy came up to Aditya and showed him a small plastic butterfly.

"Uncle, where did you get this from?" asked the boy.

"Wow, where did you find this one… this is one of the first things I collected when I started travelling. Isn't it beautiful?" said Aditya, with a huge smile on his face.

This butterfly was like his first toy in this new phase of his life. As time went by, it got buried under new ones, but never lost its place in his heart.

"Uncle, I also want to travel when I grow up," said the young boy.

"Yes, of course, you can, if that's what you want. And when you will collect your first memento, it will also hold a special place in your heart, like this one," said Aditya.

Aditya was ecstatic with the memories that rushed back, when he saw the butterfly. His first experience, the challenges and the pleasure afterwards; it was an experience that had helped him shape himself into who he was now.

After some time had passed, a man dressed in a brown suit with a white shirt tucked in and brown leather shoes came up to him. He looked around fifty years of age with a round face and a little beard. His complexion was fair and his receding hairline was noticeable. His height was average.

"Hello, young man!" he greeted Aditya with a husky voice.

"Hello sir!" Aditya greeted back.

"Nice collection, I must say." He complimented him, with a smile.

"Thank you sir," Aditya replied.

"So tell me which of these has the best story behind it?" he asked pointing towards the collection.

Aditya really liked his question. He immediately developed an admiration for the man as he was the first person to think about the collection in that manner.

"You've impressed me with your question, sir," he said with a smile.

"Well, although it is very difficult to judge and it pains me to hold one story as being better than the others – as I believe that every story is unique and magnificent in its own way – but still if you insist, then I would say that the story behind the silver Buddha is beautiful, in the way it touched someone's life and changed it for the better," Aditya continued.

"I completely agree with you when you say that every tale is magnificent in its own manner and I firmly believe that we can't judge them. However, if you have the time, I would like to hear about the story you mentioned," replied the man.

"Sure sir. Narrating the stories is pleasurable," Aditya said.

Aditya told him the entire story about Sara, despite interruptions from other people.

"Very well, young man. The biggest gift you can give to someone is raising his self-esteem and making him realise his own worth. Because unless you know your worth, you can't walk towards the path to success. I heard you when you were talking to the old woman some time back. If I am not mistaken, you were helping her deal with some problem. I have also heard that you feed stray dogs when you see them hungry. What is all this kindness for? Are you redeeming yourself or what?" he asked.

Aditya laughed and replied, "You've a sharp mind, sir. But I'm not seeking redemption. Helping others when I see them in pain gives me happiness and prevents me from feeling guilty later. Everybody looks for happiness and satisfaction in the things they do. I am no different."

The man was satisfied with his replies. He gave Aditya a pat on the shoulder and shook hands with him.

"Nice meeting you, young man. I'm John," he said.

"Nice meeting you Mr. John. I hope you know I'm Aditya," he replied in a witty tone.

"Yes, I do," he replied, smiling, and took his leave.

Soon, Rita came to congratulate Aditya on another successful event.

"Why didn't you charge people for the entry?" she asked.

"Maybe I'll think of it when I'm really broke," he replied laughing.

Rita stayed with Aditya till the end. Aditya was satisfied and elated after the success. He found solace after seeing Zinnia smiling at home while playing with Sid. He told her everything that had happened at the exhibition and she made chicken momos for him for a perfect closure of the day.

The Next Road

It was Wednesday. Rita and Aditya went to meet Samara. Samara was dressed in a frock with her hair tied in a pony. She was on a wheelchair in her room. Samara, at her age, was the prettiest girl Aditya had seen. Her golden hair and big green eyes made her look like a doll.

After taking adequate information about her medical treatment and condition from her parents, Aditya went to her room. Her parents and Rita followed him.

"Hello Samara!" Aditya greeted her.

Samara looked at her parents as if to take their permission before starting talking to a stranger and then replied, "Hello uncle!"

"How are you?" Aditya asked.

"I'm fine," she replied.

"Excited to move to a new place?" he asked further.

She didn't respond. Aditya gestured Rita to take her parents out of the room for a while.

"What happened? You'll make new friends there. Won't you like that?" He continued.

"But I'll lose my old friends. I don't want that," she replied in a low voice.

"You won't. You can always stay in touch with them through your parents' phone. You can talk to them; tell them about your new home, new friends, new school, and new life. You can exchange stories about your old friends with your new ones." He continued, when she interrupted him in between and said, "But I won't see them."

Aditya smiled and said, "You'll see them. You can see their pictures. You can talk to them too. And probably you could come back here once you've recovered. Then you'll have more friends than you have now."

Samara didn't say anything this time, so Aditya took the conversation to another angle. "What do you want to be when you grow up?"

"A teacher," she replied with a certain spark in her eyes.

Aditya was elated. Just when he was about to speak, he saw that spark fade away. "But have you seen a teacher on a wheelchair? I won't even be able to stand up and write on the blackboard," she added.

"Who said that? Did your doctor say that?" he asked.

"No. but I fall down whenever I try to stand," she said.

"Who is your favourite teacher at school?" he asked.

"Anisha ma'am."

"Do you want to be like her?" he asked.

She nodded.

"Samara, tell me, didn't you fall down when you were small?

Did you immediately start walking and running the day you were born?" he asked.

"No," she replied.

"You took time to learn, right?" he asked.

She nodded.

"Then why can't you learn now? Why can't you take time now? If you can't walk now, that's fine. That doesn't mean you'll never walk. I too fall down and hurt myself. But I walk again. Yes, it takes time. Maybe days, weeks… sometimes even months. But I do walk again." He tried to convince her.

"Samara, look at me and answer me truthfully. Do you want to run again?" he asked.

"Yes," she replied.

"Do you have the courage to fight your own battles?" he asked.

"Yes," she replied.

"Are you determined to be like Anisha ma'am?" he asked.

"Yes," she replied.

"Then remember my words. YOU WILL DO IT. Now take my hand and try to stand up," he said.

"I'll fall down," she said.

"Are you scared of falling down? Isn't this a battle? You said you were courageous," he said. "Now take my hand."

He gave Samara his full support and made her stand up. He held her with both hands and shared her load.

"How does it feel now? Are you scared even now? Or do you feel good?" he asked.

"I feel good," she answered.

"Now tell me, what's making you different from Anisha ma'am?" he asked.

She looked up at him. "You're standing. You could write if there was a blackboard. It's just the steps that are missing. The steps you take to and fro while writing on the board," he said.

He made her sit and asked, "Have you seen a butterfly?"

"Yes," she said.

"Isn't it beautiful?" he asked. She nodded.

"Do you know what a caterpillar is?" he asked.

"Yes. It turns into the butterfly," she replied.

"Have you seen a caterpillar flying?" he asked.

"No," she answered.

"So my dear, you don't know what you could transform into, if you don't try. You could run just like a butterfly could fly, if you have the courage to break free from your fears just like the caterpillar. If you can stand, then you can take a few steps too. If you do that, you can walk a mile. If you can walk a mile, you can run. And you've already seen that you can stand. So there's no stopping you unless you want your fears to rule you. Yes, you'll fall down. I am not saying you won't fall down. Yes, you'll get disheartened. But no caterpillar can transform into a butterfly without hurting itself first," he said.

A little smile seemed to be breaking on her lips when he asked, "Now tell me what do you want to be?"

"A butterfly," she replied, smiling.

"Yes, you're going to a new place, but you'll get better there. Never underestimate yourself. Take the steps that are missing right now. Will you?" he asked.

"Yes, I will," she replied.

"The next time I see you, I want to see you run."

She nodded.

He kissed her on her cheeks, met her family before leaving and left with Rita. He told Rita what happened.

"Will power matters a lot in such cases. I just wanted to make sure she doesn't lose out on her will power." He explained to Rita.

Rita started admiring him even more from that moment onwards.

After his show came to an end on Saturday, Aditya stepped down the stage to meet Zinnia, Sid and Rita. He saw Mr. John on the way. They greeted each other and Mr. John invited him for dinner at the same place. He accepted the offer and conveyed the message to all three of them. They left the venue and Aditya went to Mr. John's table.

"He sings well," said the owner.

"Yes, he does," replied Mr. John.

"Aditya, I and Mr. John are old friends. We have had some amazing times together. I am sure you'll like meeting him," said the owner.

"I already met him once and I like him already," he replied.

All three of them laughed and the owner left them to chat.

"So young man, what other talents do you possess?" Mr. John started the conversation.

As soon as he said this, Samara and her parents came up to Aditya. Her mother said, "We are leaving for Siliguri tomorrow. We thought we should see your performance before leaving. Besides, Samara wanted to thank you for that day."

Aditya turned to Samara and said, "Hello young lady! You're looking very pretty."

"Thank you uncle! I feel much better after you motivated me that day. Your words have inspired me a lot. I promise you that you'll see me running the next time we meet," she said.

He hugged Samara. He was too overwhelmed to say anything further.

"We should go now. You performed really well. We are delighted to have come here," Samara's father said.

Aditya promised to meet Samara again and waved her goodbye.

"So whatever I heard about you was correct. You really are a messiah for the distressed. We need men like you," said Mr. John.

"I am no messiah. I have done nothing great," Aditya replied.

"So, who are you? Tell me about yourself," said, Mr. John.

Aditya narrated his story and Mr. John was rather impressed.

"Actually Aditya, I had a work for you. I needed your help. I have been observing you since a long time. I am sure you could sort out my problem. I don't doubt your ability to cheer people up and instil confidence in them," said Mr. John.

"Sure sir. How can I help you?" he asked.

"I am a businessman. I have my own tea estates here. I have a sister who lives in Sikkim, not very far from here. Her daughter is about twenty-two years of age. She fell in love with a boy who couldn't survive cancer. They had been childhood friends and later on they became more than that. He's been dead for a year now, but she hasn't been able to accept his death. She has gone into depression. She doesn't talk to anyone. She remains aloof and doesn't have any friends left. I want you to be her friend, talk to her and bring her back to life."

"But how can I do that? I don't know her, then why would she listen to me?" Aditya said.

"Did you know that old woman? Or Samara? Or that girl who gave you that Buddha? You didn't, yet you changed their lives. Look son, I have observed you very keenly. I know you can do this. That little girl is very dear to us. We can't lose her like that. Please help us," he replied.

"I'll try to help you sir. I'll do the best I can. What's her name?" Aditya replied.

"Her name is Jacqueline," Mr. John told him.

"I want you to move to Sikkim at the earliest. You can live as a tenant at my sister's home. You won't have to pay rent or for food. We'll take care of that. We can even provide you with facilities which you would require to explore Sikkim. You can go anywhere you like and explore the place. This way you'll get a new place to travel to and you'll also help us out. Alright?" He continued.

"I have a contract to perform here every Saturday for a month. A couple of weeks are still left. I am staying as a tenant here. My bond is to expire on Tuesday, which I thought I would renew, since I am not done with Darjeeling yet," Aditya explained his position.

"Hmm… See, we can do one thing. I'll talk to the owner. He's my dear friend and he'll agree to pay you for your performances till today. I'll pay you whatever is remaining. You don't renew your bond for tenancy on Tuesday. You can leave for Sikkim. I'll arrange everything," he said.

"You don't have to pay me anything. I'll even pay my rent in Sikkim. I'll help you regardless," he said.

"No son. Please don't pay rent or for food there. Let us do something for you in return, otherwise we would be forever in your debt. Please, son," Mr. John requested.

He talked to the owner about the contract, who paid Aditya his due.

"How long am I to say there?" Aditya asked.

"Till she recovers or you feel you can't help her more."

Things were finalised between them and Aditya left for his house.

After entering the house, he went straight to Zinnia in the kitchen. He enquired about Mrs. Anita and then told her about what had happened.

"I am sure you'll be able to help her. You are a great influencer," she said.

"I have to leave on Tuesday," he said.

"Would you never come back?" she asked.

"I will. I don't know when. It could take a few months or more. Till she recovers," he answered.

Zinnia looked sad. She didn't want him to go.

"Sid will miss you," she said.

"I'll miss all of you too," he replied.

"Zinnia, before I leave, I wanted to know if everything is fine between you and your mom. Forgive me, but I overheard your conversation that day when you had asked for her permission to go out and when there was some problem with the food. She spoke to you very harshly." He showed his concern for her.

"She just has a bad temper. It's nothing. Don't worry," she assured him.

Aditya felt a bit relieved.

"I am not done with this place yet. I'll surely come back," he reassured her.

She smiled.

Zinnia couldn't sleep that night. She had developed an inexplicable attachment for him. The thought of him leaving left her dismayed. On the other hand, Aditya felt he was leaving a part of himself in Darjeeling. He would be incomplete without it, and for it, he must come back.

On Tuesday morning, Aditya left. Rita, Sid and Zinnia gathered for his farewell. Aditya and Zinnia spoke to each other through their eyes and not words. They both were too drained to say anything. They felt weak emotionally and physically, but the decision had been made.

Aditya reached Sikkim in a few hours. Mr. John couldn't accompany him due to some commitments, but had made all the arrangements.

On reaching the Joseph Mansion, Aditya met Jacqueline's parents. They were quite friendly. They told him about Rohan, Jacqueline's lost love and how her condition had deteriorated day by day after his death. They showed him his room after that. He was later served with tea and snacks.

The next morning, Aditya found Jacqueline sitting on a bench in the garden, looking at flowers. She was lost in herself. Her black eyes looked deep. Her gaze was in perfect synchronization with the pain inside her. Melancholy could be seen all over her face.

Aditya noticed her sharp nose and black curly hair. He couldn't take his eyes off her face. He could see sadness even in the curves of her slight smile, which would appear for a second while she was engrossed in her thoughts, signalling that she was starting her day with happy memories. Aditya could feel her pain, the pain of losing a loved one. Hiding his own pain behind a chirpy voice, he said, "Hey! I'm Aditya, your new tenant."

She looked at him in fury as if he had disturbed her in the middle of something of great importance. Then she stood up and walked past him, completely ignoring what he had said. She went inside the house without acknowledging his presence in the garden.

From that moment, Aditya knew that he was going to have a really difficult time reaching her.

Healing

A ditya tried to talk to Jacqueline, looking for an opportunity the entire day, but couldn't. She would stay inside her room and keep the door locked for long hours. Her food would be served in her room. He kept waiting, but she didn't come out of her room.

"You see her condition? She remains lost the entire day. She was so full of life earlier and now she just stays inside as if she would have herself buried there," commented her mother and started crying as soon as she spoke the last word. She ran towards her room.

Aditya could empathise with her.

The next morning, Aditya saw Jacqueline sitting on the same bench in the garden, gazing at the same flowers, like the day before. He took a deep breath and walked towards her.

He sat on the other side of the bench, and asked, "Can you suggest some fun places that I could visit here? I am new here."

She turned towards him and gave him a tight slap on his left cheek. Her parents were standing at the door to listen to their conversation. They saw what she did. Her mother put her hand on her mouth in utter surprise at her reaction. Aditya was shaken. He felt helpless. He couldn't understand how he would be able to gain her trust if she wouldn't talk to him. She rose and went inside the house, her parents still standing at the door. Aditya kept sitting there. He was in shock, his thoughts scrambled.

"I told John that this is not going to work. Nobody can help her. We have lost her," Mrs. Joseph cried.

Mr. Joseph took her inside.

With renewed courage, Aditya asked Mrs. Joseph to allow him to take dinner for Jacqueline to her room instead of the servant. She agreed. He held the tray and knocked at the door. She opened it. As soon as she saw him, she threw the tray away from his hand. The food lay on the floor. Aditya took a step back. He couldn't understand the reason for her anger towards him. Mrs. Joseph couldn't bear to see her daughter in such a state. She ran towards her, but she locked the door of her room. She didn't eat anything that night.

Mrs. Joseph didn't want her daughter's condition to deteriorate further. She discussed the matter with her husband and both of them decided to talk to Mr. John and ask him to call Aditya back.

Aditya too didn't have dinner that night. He lay in his bed, numb. He couldn't think of alternatives. His thoughts were messed up. He didn't realise when he fell asleep.

The next morning, he decided that he wouldn't go near Jacqueline. He feared that seeing him could affect her mental health adversely. He had breakfast in his room and went outside to explore Sikkim. Meanwhile, the Josephs had talked to Mr. John and had decided to give Aditya at least a week. Aditya was exhausted when he came back. His mind was burdened regarding Jacqueline's condition. By night, he had started missing his own family. He longed to see his parents and grandparents. Lost in his thoughts, he picked up his guitar and sitting at the entrance of the house, he started playing music of the song which his grandfather used to sing for his grandmother. The music was slow and touching. As he played his guitar, his sadness grew further.

Jacqueline heard the sound of his guitar. She became enchanted to the music. It drew her towards itself, as if it had cast a spell on her. She came out of her room and stood at the door for a few minutes. As Aditya continued to play, she walked towards him and stood by his side. He looked at her, stopped playing and rose.

"I know you are trying to impress me with this music. How did you come to know about this song? Why are you playing mental games with me?" she spoke in a mellowed tone.

It was the first time she had spoken to him. The music had subsided her anger and brought her pain to her lips.

"I don't know what you are talking about. I was missing my grandparents, so I chose to play their favourite song. I have lost them now. I was just reliving those days," he explained.

She started crying and sat at the door. Aditya sat beside her. He didn't say anything. He wanted her to cry as much as she could, for he thought that would subside her anger and pain. Only when she has cried to the fullest can she learn to smile again, he thought.

"Rohan…Rohan…," she started shouting while crying. All the pain she had locked up inside was coming onto the surface. Hearing her cry, her parents came out. Her mother calmed her down. Aditya asked her to let her cry. But Mrs. Joseph couldn't take it anymore and took Jacqueline to her room.

The next morning, the Josephs called Aditya to their room.

"Considering Jacqueline's condition since you have come, we have decided to only give you a week. Today is your fourth day. You have only seventy-two hours after today. If we see a ray of hope by then, then you'll stay here, otherwise you'll have to leave. I hope you understand our situation as parents," Mr. Joseph declared.

Aditya nodded, gave a fake smile and left the room. As he was walking towards his room, he saw Jacqueline standing at a distance.

"Can you play that music again?" she asked.

Aditya was both happy and scared.

"Sure, I can, but I don't want you to get hurt. It ended up pretty badly last night," he answered.

She didn't say anything and turned around to walk away. Aditya called out from behind.

"Hey, wait! I'll bring my guitar. Please wait for me in the garden," he said.

She nodded without turning around.

Aditya took his guitar and went to the garden. He saw her sitting on the bench.

"May I sit here?" he asked.

She nodded in the affirmative.

He sat beside her and started playing. She closed her eyes and listened to the music. Then she opened them and started gazing at the red roses. After Aditya finished playing, he asked her, "Do you know how to play the guitar?"

"No," she answered.

"Do you want to learn?" he asked.

"Yes. Can you teach me?" she asked back.

"Yes, of course. When do you want to start?" he asked.

"Right now," she answered.

"Sure then," he said.

He smiled and started teaching her from scratch.

"Can you give me lessons every day?" she asked, when she was done for the time being.

"Yes, sure. Whenever you say," he answered.

She nodded and got up to go to her room.

Aditya left for the Orchid sanctuary after that. When he came back in the evening, he saw Jacqueline standing at the gate.

"Where were you? I had been waiting for my lessons the entire day," she said.

"I am sorry I didn't know we had to meet again today. I had gone to the Orchid sanctuary," he answered.

"I want to learn to play the guitar as soon as possible so that I can play that song. Can we have our next lesson right now?" she asked.

"Okay. I'll just freshen up and meet you here. Meanwhile, please be ready with a pen and a paper to take notes," he said.

She nodded and both of them went to their rooms. They met at the same place after twenty minutes. Aditya started off with the second lesson. The Josephs were really happy to see that. Aditya had done what nobody had been able to do – he had aroused in her the desire to do something.

After the lesson got over, they decided to meet in the garden the next morning.

"Can you teach me the whole day tomorrow? I want to learn this as fast as possible," she said.

"Alright. I won't go anywhere tomorrow. I'll give you lessons for as long as you want," he said.

They started off by rehearsing the lessons of the previous day the next morning. Apart from a few minor corrections, Jacqueline had done pretty well.

"You are a quick learner. It's just been a day. You are taking this seriously. Great!" Aditya complimented her.

He expected her to smile, but she started looking down.

They started off with the next lesson. After an hour, they took a break.

"We never had a tenant till now. Then how are you living with us?" she asked.

"Umm…well, your uncle Mr. John and I are really good friends. We are very close to each other. I had some work here, which can take a few months. Since I know nobody here, he asked me to stay as a tenant with her sister," he lied, partly.

She nodded.

"I can't wait to play the song on the guitar," she said with a twinkle in her eye.

Aditya smiled and asked, "It's such an old song. How do you like it the most and not any current one ?"

"Sometimes things get associated with a lot of memories. You like them even more because they bring with them a plethora of good memories. They don't remain mere things then, they serve as memoirs," she said staring blankly into open space.

"That's true. That song is indeed special, I suppose. It holds something special for both of us," he said, smiling. She kept staring and didn't respond.

"Well, to play the song, you'll have to learn the basics first. Once you do that right, you can play it. And also any other song you may wish to play," he added.

Mr. and Mrs. Joseph were really happy to see her like that. They called Mr. John and informed him about the development. Mr. John had never doubted Aditya's capabilities and his heart filled with pride to have chosen a guy like him for the purpose.

Slowly, Jacqueline started getting comfortable around Aditya. The guitar lessons had given way to friendship between them. But Jacqueline hadn't smiled even then.

It was one fine evening when Aditya had come back from Lachen. Lately he had started missing Zinnia a lot, so he took a break to visit Lachen so that he could regain his focus on the task assigned to him.

Jacqueline saw Aditya entering the house. She opened her mouth as to call him, but stopped as soon as she realised that she didn't know his name. She chucked away the thought and called out, "Hey! You back?"

"Hello, Jacqueline. How are you doing?" Aditya replied, walking towards her.

"I am great. How was Lachen?" she asked.

"It's so pretty. It is like heaven on earth. The crystal clear water, those valleys, the vegetation and flowers! I loved it so much! The perfect getaway," he replied.

"I missed my guitar lessons. Had nothing to do the entire day," she said.

"Don't worry! We're gonna start tomorrow," he replied.

Mr. and Mrs. Joseph welcomed him. He dozed off soon after having dinner.

The next morning, he met Jacqueline in the garden.

"Ready?" he asked, sitting on the bench.

"Yes."

"Okay, then. Show me a glimpse of whatever we have practised till now," he said in a commanding tone.

She did as instructed.

"Oh my god, Jacqueline! You're too good. Tell me you practised while I was gone," he said.

She laughed.

Aditya was the happiest person to see her laugh that way. She laughed just like a child does when he knows he has been caught. Because the previous day she had said that she had nothing to do the entire day, while the way she played the guitar clearly showed otherwise. She laughed whole-heartedly, unforcefully, mischievously, just like a little child. Aditya wished her parents could see her laughing like that. He felt the same as a father would on seeing his child laugh after many days have passed. He felt satiated. His efforts had started paying off.

He laughed with her and teased her, "Of course you did nothing the entire day!"

"Enough stranger! What's your name, by the way? I realised just yesterday that I didn't even know your name," she said.

"Aditya," he replied, smiling.

He teased her again by standing up, putting his hand forward and introducing himself.

"Hello ma'am! I am Aditya. Nice to meet you."

"Okay Aditya. Now start the lessons," she said, emphasizing on his name.

They started off with the lessons.

When they were stopping for the day, Aditya said, "You're good to start with the song tomorrow. Hopefully, we'll do half of it."

The next day when Jacqueline could play half of the song on the guitar, Aditya said, "Just a bit of practice and then you'll play it like a professional. We'll ask your parents to listen to it once we're done with the full song."

She smiled.

Aditya was reminded of Zinnia's first smile on seeing hers. He was lost in Zinnia's thoughts when Jacqueline interrupted.

"Hey, where are you lost?"

"Nothing," he answered, blushing.

"Look, someone's blushing! Hey, are you in love?" she asked.

"I'm not blushing," he said.

"Of course, you are! Now tell me everything," she said.

"I have never seen you so curious!" he said.

"Well, now you have. Come on now, speak up!" She urged.

"Yes, I am…" he blushed again.

"Carry on," she said.

"Her name is Zinnia. I don't know if it's love. I mean, I have this weird sweet feeling inside me which I have never felt before. I am anxious to meet her, talk to her and just see her from a distance. I miss her voice. I missed her in Lachen. I miss her every damn time! I don't know, but from the moment I met her, I never wanted to go away from her. You know, she's different from the rest. It's not that I haven't had crushes before; I have liked many girls. But this sweet pain, the sweet agony which I am feeling now, I swear I haven't felt it before." He blurted out all his feelings.

"And yet after describing it so much, I don't feel I have been able to do justice to what I am truly feeling inside," he added.

"Oh, oh, oh... My teacher is in love!" she teased.

"Where does she live?" she asked.

"Darjeeling," he answered.

"So, why don't you just tell her about how you feel?" she asked.

"I will. When I go to Darjeeling, I will," he said.

"And when will that happen?" she asked.

"After I finish off my work here," he said.

"And what's that? I never see you going to work," she said.

"Miss Jacqueline, I know you're very curious, but I'm hungry. Let's go and eat something," he said changing the subject.

"Panchii...Panchii...," she called out to her servant.

"Why are you calling her? We'll go eat inside," he said.

"No, no. The weather's nice. We'll eat here," she said.

"Panchi, please get us some vegetable sandwiches?" she said.

"Okay ma'am." The servant went away to get them.

"So, what's your story?" he asked her.

"Did I upset you? I'm sorry I didn't mean to," he said, seeing the sudden change of expression on her face.

"No, it's okay," she responded.

"If you don't want to share anything, that's fine," he said.

"What are you saying?! We're friends!" she said.

"Happy to hear that!" he said, smiling. She smiled back.

After a few minutes of silence, she continued.

"I loved someone. In fact, I love him even now. His name was Rohan. We were childhood friends. He had lung cancer. We knew that he wouldn't survive it, but we hoped that he did. But, he didn't. It's been a year now. I wasn't ready to let him go. I knew that he would go away, but I could never accept it. Not even now. I have spent my entire childhood with him. He understood me the way nobody ever can. He knew me so well. He knew what I wanted, how, when, how I feel at different times, he knew me from inside and out. He knew my best and the worst side and he still accepted me. I could be myself with him, unapologetically. I would never have a companion like him and I can't afford to lose him. Even now he's with me. He's in my heart, in the breath I take, inside me, in the air, everywhere! I can't leave him. I want to stay with him. He can't leave me." She vented out her emotions.

"Jacqueline...calm down!" he said, putting his hand on her head.

"You know, you don't have to leave him," he said.

She looked at him in surprise.

"Yes. You can continue loving him. He can be inside you. If you want him to stay with you, then let him. Nobody's taking him away. He can be in your heart and memories. He can be your muse, your guiding spirit and your companion. He can accompany you everywhere. But only inside you," he said.

She kept looking at him.

"I have lost my family, but they're still with me all the time. Their guidance, values, memories, love... stay with me wherever I go. They encourage me. They urge me to live. You know, death is natural. It has to happen today or tomorrow but when your dear ones die, they can still stay with you," he said.

"Tell me Jacqueline. Did Rohan ever tell you to stop living when he's gone?" he asked.

"No... he knew about his illness, so he used to discuss the future often with me," she said.

"So what did he want?" he asked.

"He wanted me to be happy. He wanted me to settle down with someone else. The latter was his last wish. But tell me Aditya, how can I do it?" She cried.

"Jacqueline, it's entirely up to you. I am not saying that you have to fulfil his last wish at any cost and go get yourself a husband. The thing is, that you have to start living. I know you feel that there's no reason left, but Rohan has given you the biggest reason himself. He wanted you to live happily after he's gone. The life which he couldn't live, you have to live!

"You can't waste it just like that. It would be an insult to him. He couldn't save himself, but he would have if he could, to stay with you. Now you have to save yourself to let him stay with you, in your memories, and live for him. You've to live like how he would've lived, otherwise you would not only insult his love for you, but also disregard what he wanted. If he had discussed all this often, then I am sure he wanted you to do as he wanted. If you don't do that, you would disrespect him. You know how am I making my family happy after their death? By living the life of my choice, because I know they would have wanted the same," he said.

She was staring at something he didn't turn to see. "Jacqueline, I am not asking you to hunt for a lover. I am asking you to give yourself a chance. Start living normally. If you find love again, that's great, and if you don't, it doesn't matter. If you can't fulfil his last wish now, maybe you can do that later. Maybe you'll get that chance. When you feel that you're ready to live with someone, look for a partner. You don't have to find him yourself. Your parents can. If you feel you can't love again then go for an arranged marriage when you're ready for it. Take your time. You can either live alone or with someone, but you've to live! And not just exist." He made her understand.

"You're a strong girl, Jacqueline. And Rohan's love can make you stronger. Fight yourself because disrespecting what he wanted would be far worse. Fight for him." He encouraged her.

"Will you?" he asked.

She nodded.

"I know I might have repeated things which others might have already said. You might have heard all this many times before, but this is the way how things should be," he said.

"You can feel my pain. You have also suffered by losing your loved ones. I didn't think people could relate to me earlier. But you can," she said.

A strange silence hung over them. Jacqueline was thinking of what Aditya had just said, and Aditya was feeling overwhelmed with her pain. Soon, Panchi came with sandwiches. They ate them and went to their rooms.

Jacqueline felt better after sharing her pain with Aditya. Aditya felt better after showing her the right path, but he was dedicated more than ever to turn his words into action.

Soon, Jacqueline made her parents listen to her while she played the entire song on the guitar. They were overwhelmed on seeing their daughter play so well. Mrs. Joseph hugged her tightly when she finished playing. Mr. Joseph gave her a kiss on the forehead. The Josephs were delighted to see their daughter recovering. They couldn't thank Aditya enough.

Mr. John would talk to Aditya on phone often. Meanwhile, Rita would ask Mr. John about Aditya and gave updates to Zinnia and Sid. Indirectly, Zinnia would know about the progress and pray for him. Without Aditya knowing about it, Zinnia would know how he was, what he was doing, how far he had progressed and about the places he visited.

Bringing Jacqueline back to life required constant efforts from Aditya's side. He needed to repeatedly encourage her. The process of revitalising her soul and bring back meaning to her life took time and demanded patience.

"I want to see a glacier." Aditya said one day.

"Okay." Jacqueline replied.

"But I don't want to go trekking alone. Will you accompany me if your parents allow?" he asked.

"Come on! I taught you how to play a guitar," he added, seeing her hesitant.

"Oh! So now I'll have to repay you?" she asked, teasingly.

"I was joking!" he said.

"I know! Okay, I'll join you, my only friend." She agreed. They both laughed.

Though reluctant at first to send their daughter with someone they had known only for a few months, the Josephs agreed to let Jacqueline accompany Aditya after getting a green signal from Mr. John. Soon, Aditya and Jacqueline went trekking for a week.

During the week, they shared stories about the loves of their lives and the funny little incidents, the sweet nothings and their best moments. Aditya told her that he was a traveller and that coming to Sikkim involved both the work and the travelling part. He would divert her attention whenever she would ask about the work and laugh off her jokes about a traveller on work. He told her how weird Zinnia thought travellers were and how pretty she looked when she would say that. She told him about Rohan's family. They shared memories which meant the whole world to them. They had become better friends. They understood and knew each other better after the trek. Jacqueline started trusting him even more after those seven days. The Rathong glacier was the one place they were going to remember forever, both for its beauty and its memories. Not only was the path to the glacier a repository of the secrets of nature, but also the secrets of the hearts which they both shared with each other on the way. Although the trek was really difficult, but the stories they shared with each other made the journey easy. The beauty of the place got amalgamated with the beauty of the sweet memories and the journey became heavenly.

When they came back, they met Rohan's family – his younger sister and parents.

Aditya encouraged Jacqueline to do what Rohan would have done for his family. She took a pledge to always take care of his family and be the elder sister to his younger sister. She would help them in all ways possible and became the second daughter of the house. Aditya reminded her how much her parents loved and cared for her. He told her about what they had been going through and how their life too would lose meaning without her love. From then onwards, Jacqueline started spending more time with her family and helped her father in his business. Being the only child of the house, she promised her parents that she would take over her father's business. She had started accepting love from her dear ones.

Aditya's work was done. It was time for him to leave. He told Jacqueline that he would be leaving in a week.

"Why are you going? You can stay with us! I need you!" she said on hearing that.

"I had to go someday. I have to go to Zinnia," he said.

"Why can't you bring her here?" she asked.

"She has a family there. I can't do that," he answered.

"God! I don't want you to go. Promise me that you'll keep meeting me and always stay in touch," she said, hugging him.

"I'll get you a phone to stay in touch," she added.

They both laughed.

Rita got to know that Aditya was coming back through Mr. John. Zinnia started preparing in advance by cleaning the room properly and working on an embroidered handkerchief for him. He was coming back after three months. In these three months, Zinnia had rejected four potential tenants by telling them that the place was booked. Though scared of Mrs. Anita's wrath, she did it because love gave her the courage. On three occasions, she had encountered the tenants when she was alone or working in the garden. On the fourth one, she had to take Sid's help by making him convince Mrs. Anita that he didn't like the tenant. Mrs. Anita would do nothing to displease Sid and Sid was always more than happy to do something for Aditya. Rita asked Mr. John to tell Aditya that he could stay with Zinnia and Sid again as the room was still vacant. When Aditya got the news, he jumped with excitement and waited impatiently for that day to arrive when he would see Zinnia again.

On the day when he was leaving, Jacqueline gave Aditya a mobile phone to stay in touch and a Buddhist artefact as a memoir. She cried when he was leaving and promised to always follow the path he had shown her. He asked her to call him whenever she needed help. She did the same.

The Josephs gave him a warm farewell and asked him to tell them whenever he needed help of any sort.

"I can't offer you money because that would be insulting. But please tell me if you need something. I will help you in whichever way possible," said Mr. Joseph.

"You gave me your house to live in, food to eat, helped me explore this amazing place and gave me a friend for life. I don't need anything else," he said.

The Josephs gave him a pat on the back. Aditya had won hearts again!

Everybody bade him farewell.

Avowal

Aditya reached Darjeeling at night. He went to Mrs. Anita's house directly. Mrs. Anita opened the door and asked him to come in.

"So, you've come back?" she asked.

"Yes. Is the room still vacant?" he asked. He already knew the answer.

"It's vacant. You can stay there again. How was Sikkim, by the way?" she asked.

"Good. Sikkim is very beautiful," he answered.

"I thought you won't come back. I mean, you're a traveller. I thought you would go to some new place after that," she said.

"Actually I had gone to Sikkim for some work. I wasn't done with Darjeeling in just a month, and I will go to Sikkim again. I haven't explored it my way yet. There are many things left," he said.

"Oh!" she exclaimed.

"So, where's Sid? I can't see him around," he said.

"He's gone outside with Zinnia for a walk," she replied.

She observed his reaction on the mention of Zinnia, but his face didn't give away his feelings.

"Okay then. You may go to your room. It's clean. I'll inform Sid that you have come back when he returns. I am sure he missed you," she said smiling.

He smiled back and went to his room.

He set his room, put the artefact in his box and took out the mobile phone. He switched on the phone and saw a message from Jacqueline, *"Happy Journey!"*

He should have switched it on earlier, he thought.

Soon, Sid came back with Zinnia. His mother told him about Aditya. He went to the kitchen to inform Zinnia about the same and urged her to take him to Aditya's room. She blushed on hearing the news and took him to Aditya's room. Before she could knock, Sid ran ecstatically inside the room.

"Sid!" She entered the room calling him.

Sid jumped onto Aditya's lap. Aditya looked up. Zinnia blushed on seeing him. Aditya realised that and blushed in response.

"Welcome back, uncle!" Sid greeted him.

"How are you, my boy? Come Zinnia, sit!" he addressed both of them.

Zinnia sat beside them.

"How was your stay at Sikkim? And how is that girl now?" she asked.

"It was good. Jacqueline feels much better now. I hope she stays that way," he replied.

"Look Zinnia, uncle's got a phone! What else did you bring, uncle?" asked Sid.

"Jacqueline gave me this to stay in touch." He told them.

He asked Sid to pass him the wooden box and showed them the artefact. They loved it.

"When did you come?" Zinnia asked.

"About an hour ago," he replied.

"You must be hungry. I'll bring you something to eat," she said.

"It's okay Zinnia. Sit with us for some time," he said.

"We've had dinner. Let me get you something too. We have time to talk, but I don't want you to stay hungry," she said, getting up. They couldn't talk much later. Aditya had dinner and all of them went to sleep.

As soon as Aditya heard Mrs. Anita going out of the house the next day, he immediately got out of his room to talk to Zinnia.

"Hi!" he greeted her.

"Hi!" she greeted back.

"Won't you like to know what I did in the last three months?" he asked.

She smirked at him. Little did he know that she knew everything.

"Let's sit in the living room," she said.

Aditya told her everything. He made her visualise everything through his incredible narrating skills. It looked to Zinnia as if she had gone along with him. He always surprised her with his talents.

"So Jacqueline would keep calling you now?" she asked.

He could see her getting insecure.

"I guess so. I'll make you talk to her too," he said.

"Does she even know me?" she asked.

"Yes, I told her about you. We would often talk about you," he replied.

"You talked about me? Why?" she asked.

He blushed.

"Zinnia... I want to tell you something. Do you have more time?" he asked.

"I think it's time to pick Sid up from school. Is it urgent?" she replied.

He looked upset.

"We have ten minutes," she said on seeing him upset.

"Chuck it. You can pick Sid up from school. We'll talk later," he said getting up.

What he wanted to say would have required more than just ten minutes. He didn't want to say anything in a hurry. He wanted some alone time with her, but he knew he wouldn't get it once Sid came back. Disappointed, he went inside his room. He cursed himself for not telling his feelings first as he had ample time earlier. He could have narrated the Sikkim tales later. Thinking that he had lost a golden opportunity, he went outside to get fresh air when Sid came back. He didn't want to talk to anyone at that time because he was angry with himself. And he knew that Sid would definitely seek his company.

He visited a lake, ate noodles there and sat beside the water for hours. He observed the ripples in the water, the ponies giving rides to people and the landscape.

When he came back, Mrs. Anita was already home. He went to his room quietly.

Zinnia was extremely worried due to his behaviour. She thought that he had felt bad that she couldn't spare enough time for him.

In the morning, she lied to Mrs. Anita, "Sid was complaining yesterday that you and father never drop him to school. So why don't you drop him today? He'll feel good."

"Was he really saying that?" Mrs. Anita asked back.

Zinnia nodded. She believed her.

Mrs. Anita called her husband and together they went to Sid's school.

As soon as they left the house, Zinnia knocked on Aditya's door. He had woken up by then, but was not completely awake. He opened the door rubbing his eyes. Zinnia called him out.

"Hey, are you mad at me?" she asked.

"No, why?" he asked back.

"You didn't talk to me yesterday and went away just like when I mentioned that I need to pick Sid up from school," she explained.

He laughed.

"No, I am not mad at you," he said.

"Then, tell me, why did you behave like that?" she asked.

"Because I act stupid at times," he replied.

"And what was it you wanted to say?" she asked.

"You are hurling questions at me early in the morning! I haven't even woken up properly yet and you expect me to propose to you in this state!" he said and smirked immediately after.

"What!" she exclaimed.

She kept looking at him in surprise.

"I just thought that a casual start would be cool," he said.

She kept staring at him without blinking.

"Sit Zinnia." He made her sit on the sofa.

"So do we have time now?" he asked.

She nodded.

"Okay, so let me start this without making a fuss about the entire matter because doing that makes me really nervous. You just listen to me and don't ask questions in between. Okay?" he said.

"Okay," she replied.

"So… Zinnia. I think I'm in love with you. I've never felt this weird ever before. The feeling that you give me is out of this world. I have been travelling alone for years now and I never needed any companion, but after meeting you, I don't want to go anywhere alone. You're on my mind, every time. When I was in Sikkim, I longed to see you and hear your voice. I want you to accompany me everywhere. I have had crushes on girls before, but they didn't make me go crazy like you do. When I was leaving, I felt that my energy had been sapped, someone took a part of me away, the part which defined me, which I loved the most, and for the first time in my life, I wasn't ecstatic about going to a new place.

I care about you way too much to leave you. I want to comfort, support, and help, and be with you forever. You've made me explore a completely different side of myself. Till now, I had been exploring people, places and lives. I had been sharing journeys with people. I was being a part of so many stories. But you have made me explore myself, my feelings and what I want.

You have made me embark on a completely uncharted path and in this journey, I need you to be my partner. I don't want to be a part of this story, but I want us to write this story together," he said.

This time he had done justice to his innermost feelings. Zinnia was ecstatic, overwhelmed, surprised and confused, all at once.

"Aditya… I don't know what to say. I mean, I understand how you're feeling right now. I missed you so damn much. We got news from Mr. John about you, but I craved to meet you and hear your voice. I didn't like doing anything when you went away. I admire, respect and like you as a person. I get worried when you don't talk to me properly. I get insecure when you mention other girls. I have never seen such a kind soul before. You're too good to be real. It killed me to stay away from you. I like to be around you. I…," she stopped.

A tear rolled down Aditya's cheek on listening to her confession.

"I want to hug you right now," he said.

"Then do it," she said.

They hugged for a microsecond but had to part because they heard someone coming.

It was one of their neighbours. She had come to meet Mrs. Anita and decided to stay till she came back. Aditya went to his room and Zinnia sat to give the neighbour company.

In the evening, Mrs. Anita sent Zinnia to get groceries. Hearing that, Aditya ran outside the house to meet Zinnia on the way.

"Zinnia," he called out from behind.

"What are you doing here?" she asked.

"Looking for a chance to talk to you," he replied.

They kept walking.

"Aditya, if people see us together, they'll assume that there's something between us. If that happens, then they'll question our staying in the same house too, especially when we are alone in the house." She explained.

"So is there no place where nobody recognises us?" he asked.

"Everyone knows everyone else here. It's a small town. Plus, people recognise you too," she said.

"I understand. Okay then, I'll meet you in the house," he said.

They changed paths after that.

Aditya wasn't getting a proper chance to know Zinnia. He wanted to talk to her and had started getting impatient. He would stay at home to seize the opportunity of talking to her whenever Mrs. Anita went away, but there were interferences. For three days, he didn't explore any new place. On the fourth day, he got a chance to talk to Zinnia when Mrs. Anita had gone for a haircut.

"So, tell me how you felt when I confessed my feelings that day?" he asked.

"Well, I reciprocated the gesture," she answered smiling.

Both of them blushed.

"Zinnia, I think we should start talking more." He paused.

He continued, "I remember that in the beginning you were not convinced with the idea of me being a traveller. How do you feel about it now?"

She kept quiet.

"Zinnia, what's wrong? Why does this subject upset you?" he asked.

"Aditya, I didn't like travellers earlier. I felt that they lack loyalty towards anything – place, people, themselves. I used to think that they are always running away and that all of them are the same. But after knowing you, I have changed my mind. You are not like that. You are different, I feel," she answered.

"I am relieved to hear that. Your silence made me nervous," he said.

"So, is everything fine between you and your mother now? Did her temper improve?" he asked.

She remained silent again.

"Something is wrong, Zinnia. Please tell me." He urged.

"Actually, you don't know my story," she said.

"Because you haven't told me yet. I have told you everything about myself. It's time for you to do the same," he said.

After a minute of silence, she began by saying, "Mrs. Anita is not my real mother. I haven't seen my real parents, actually. They tell me that my father was a traveller. He came to Darjeeling and met my mother here. They got married. But my father was too keen to go on exploring places and not stay. So one day, when I was not born yet, my father left his pregnant wife in Darjeeling and went away without telling her. My mother started getting depressed. She lived in great stress. Her pregnancy got complicated. She died while giving birth to me. Then Mrs. Anita and her husband took care of me. My father never came back. He hasn't come back till now. Probably he doesn't even know about us. And I am sure he doesn't care. Had he cared about us, he would've come to see us. This is also the reason why I hated travellers."

"I'm so sorry, Zinnia. Come here," he said and they hugged.

"Don't be sad. I am here with you. You'll never be alone." He consoled her.

"I am really grateful to Mrs. Anita. She was my mom's friend, so she and Mr. Hudson took care of me after her. My grandmother was with us too when I was very small, but she didn't keep well. Age soon caught up and she passed away. I was so small that I don't even remember her face. But Mrs. Anita turned out to be a trusted friend," she said.

"So you've never tried to find your father?" he asked.

"Nobody knows where he went. I don't know anything about him except his name," she replied.

"What's his name?" he asked.

"Alex Daniels," she said.

Aditya wanted to console her, but words failed him. "You don't want to know my mother's name?" she asked.

"Of course, I do. Tell me," he said.

"Sabrina," she said.

He saw a tear rolling down her cheek, so he changed the subject to keep her away from bad memories.

Aditya and Zinnia got closer in a couple of days. Although they didn't go out together and didn't have a normal committed life, they had started understanding each other better. Aditya would stay at home when Mrs. Anita had plans, so they could spend time together. He would sometimes accompany her to Sid's school. They would have dinner together on Saturdays after his show. Zinnia and Sid would spend quality time in Aditya's room. Zinnia had told Rita about their mutual confessions. Rita was happy for Zinnia because she knew that unlike her, Zinnia was serious about Aditya and that she had confessed love for someone for the first time. Zinnia was a one-man woman and

Rita knew that unless she wanted a relationship to last till the end, she wouldn't put herself into one.

"Can I still have a crush on your hot boyfriend?" Rita asked jokingly.

"Umm... I'll think about it." Zinnia laughed.

Soon, Aditya's likes and dislikes became Zinnia's likes and dislikes, and hers became his. She would fall in love with him even more when he would start talking. She loved his ideas, stories and thoughts. He would fall in love with her whenever she would roll her eyes, get angry and laugh her heart out.

"I also like to visit new places, but I don't know if I can do that for my entire life," she said.

"But if you like it, then maybe I'll do that, but you need to stay at one place for a longer duration, like in years, so that we have at least some stability and that would be good for the kids too," she said.

"As you say, ma'am. And did you mention kids? So you want to have kids with me?" he asked.

"Not at all. I was just giving you a piece of advice," she said.

They both laughed.

She had also given him the embroidered handkerchief that she had made for him. He used to keep it with him always, under his pillow while sleeping and in his pocket otherwise.

One day Sid requested Mrs. Anita to let him go to the zoo with Aditya. He wouldn't agree when she refused and urged her again and again. Mrs. Anita had no option left. She decided to go with them and also take Zinnia along to take care of Sid. Mrs. Anita was too concerned about Sid and wouldn't send him alone with Zinnia and Aditya. That day, Aditya got his memento from Darjeeling – a wooden fish crafted beautifully. He also bought a wooden tortoise and a squirrel.

The cages were located a bit up the hill, which made reaching them difficult. When they were going to see the Red Pandas, Zinnia hurt her foot with a rock and fell down. Aditya shouted her name and ran towards her. He helped her get up and cared for her like a child. He never left her side the entire day after that. Mrs. Anita noticed all this.

The next day, Aditya had gone to meet Mr. John. He had thought that he would stay with him the entire day, but came back early because Mr. John had to go somewhere. When he came back, Zinnia had gone to pick up Sid from school. As he went towards the kitchen to check if Zinnia had come back, he heard Mrs. Anita speaking loudly in her room, "We need to do something. Do you understand?"

"So this is what you've called me for? To tell me that we need to do something about our tenant and Zinnia? And why? Because lately she's been happy!" Mr. Hudson shouted.

"It's not about her being happy. Do you even realise what people are going to say to us after that!" She shouted back.

"Oh really! As if I don't know you, Anita. Your only problem is that child's happiness. You can't see her happy. You ruined her entire life by snatching her parents from her, and now, instead of atoning for your sins, you're asking me to do something? Have you ever wondered why I don't stay in this house much? Why I am mostly outside? That is because you've made me a part of your crimes. I've started hating this house because of your malicious deeds." He vented his anger at her.

"I've taken good care of her. I have made her go to school, given her a house to live in and food to eat. Who else would have done that?" she said.

"You did it for your own cover so that people see only the good side and what you did never comes out. Nobody knows that you treat her like a servant," he said.

"Shut up, you stupid man! It was my biggest mistake to marry you. Aditya's involvement and closeness with Zinnia can be detrimental for us. We need to keep her away from everyone except the people I trust. As soon as I get a new tenant, I'll push him out of the house."

She took a deep breath and softened her voice.

"Look, we have an important matter to discuss, for which I have called you. Margarita's condition has improved a lot lately. Although she still can't get up, but her hands have shown signs of movement. I am scared that she might write something against us. We need to stop her, otherwise we'll be caught," she continued.

"What would we do to stop her?" he asked.

"That is what we need to think about. I'll go and talk to her. She can hear, but can't speak. We'll have to think of something," she said.

She sounded worried.

"I'll do something," he said.

"Now you should leave. Zinnia and Sid are about to return," she said.

Aditya rushed to his room and closed the door. He couldn't believe his ears. He could understand that there was something amiss, which was definitely not to be taken lightly. He understood that Mrs. Anita had something to do with the death of Zinnia's parents and that Mr. Hudson was also involved.

He took a pledge to find everything out.

The Conspiracy

When Zinnia came back home with Sid that day, Aditya looked for an opportunity to talk to her and fortunately got it before evening.

"Zinnia, I wanted to ask something about your parents. Can I?" He said.

"Sure."

"Who told you about what had happened?" he asked.

"Mrs. Anita and Mr. Hudson. Who else will?" she replied.

"I meant, have you ever spoken to anyone else about it?" he asked further.

"Nobody was as close to my family as Mrs. Anita and probably she's the only one who knew about the entire thing. So there's no point asking anyone else," she said.

He remained silent.

"Why did you ask me this? What's wrong?" she asked.

"Nothing. The thought just crossed my mind, so…" he replied.

"Sure?" She sought confirmation.

"Yes." He confirmed with a smile.

He called Rita to meet him in the evening at the Mall Road, now that he had a phone. Rita complied.

"Rita, I need your help." Aditya said.

"What help?" she asked.

"Do you know someone named Margarita who lives here?" he asked.

"No, I don't," she replied.

"Can you find out?" he asked.

She raised her eyebrows curiously. "Please don't ask me why I need to know about her, but just know that it's really important. It's a very serious matter and I need your help in this, no questions asked," he said.

"Okay. I won't ask. Tell me more about her," she replied.

She knew from the urgency and seriousness in his tone and on his face that the matter was indeed crucial.

"Margarita can't speak or move. Probably she's on bed for quite some time. She can hear people and lately her hand has shown signs of movement. Mrs. Anita knows her. So if someone can tell about such a woman who was in contact with Mrs. Anita, it will be of great help," he explained.

Rita had a zillion questions in her head, but kept quiet as she didn't want to upset Aditya.

"It's a small town. And I'm sure you know most of the people here. You've been living here since childhood," he said.

"Don't worry. I'll find out. I'll do my best," she replied.

"I'll get back to you as soon as I get any information," she added.

He thanked her and they went their ways. Rita had got the clue that it was somewhere related to Zinnia, but couldn't understand why Aditya was hiding it from her. Nevertheless, she was determined to help Aditya.

Days passed. Rita left no stone unturned. Aditya insisted on finding Margarita fast because he feared that Mrs. Anita would play some game and then they won't be able to get to her. But fortunately, after two days of hard work and smart thinking, Rita informed Aditya that she had found the woman.

"I found Margarita through Sonam. Sonam is Mrs. Anita's ex-maid. She and Margarita live in the same colony. When you said that she had some connection with Mrs. Anita, I began searching for all the people who had some sort of relationship with Mrs. Anita. Her neighbours told me about her maid. When Zinnia was small, Sonam used to take care of the house. She worked there for many years. But when Zinnia grew up, Mrs. Anita dismissed her because Zinnia took over. I met Sonam and asked her if she knew somebody named Margarita. Then she told me about her and I went to see her too," Rita explained on meeting Aditya.

"Go on," he said.

"Margarita used to work for Zinnia's mother, Mrs. Sabrina, as her help during her pregnancy. Margarita worked there till Mrs. Sabrina gave birth to Zinnia and sometime afterwards. Unfortunately, Zinnia lost her mother when she gave birth to her." She stopped to look at Aditya's reaction.

"Zinnia has told me everything herself. I know this. I can understand her pain. I too lost mine at a young age," he responded.

"I didn't know that she had told you," she said.

"It was just a few days ago. Anyway, so what happened after that?" he asked.

"After that, she left the job. Nobody knows why. And Mrs. Anita and Mr. Hudson and Zinnia's grandmother took care of Zinnia. But Zinnia's grandmother died after a few years because of her long lasting illness," she said.

"How is Margarita now?" he asked.

"She is paralysed. Just like you had told me; she can't move or speak but has started writing a bit. Not very clearly but she can write," she replied.

"How did she get paralysed?" he asked.

"Her daughter said that she was going somewhere at night and lost her balance. She fell down from a height and has been paralysed since then. She recovers, but then her condition worsens again. This time they didn't tell anyone about her recovery. She was shocked to know that I already knew about the improvement. Just because I was with Sonam, she agreed to make me meet her under her daughter's surveillance."

"Who all are there in her family? And why did Sonam trust you?" he asked, hoping to clear everything.

"Sonam trusted me because I am Zinnia's friend. I showed my photographs with Zinnia to her. And regarding Margarita, there's just her daughter. Her husband left her a long time ago," she answered.

"Hmm… I want to meet Margarita as soon as possible. I know it is difficult, but can you please make me meet her right now?" he asked.

"I'll try. Can't promise though. Let's go," she said.

She told him on the way that Margarita freaks out when she sees somebody entering her room, except the people she trusts.

She did freak out when Rita went inside, but Sonam had told her that she is Zinnia's friend and like her sister. Sonam showed her the photos too. Rita came out without talking to her.

"Do you have any picture with Zinnia?" she asked him.

"No," he said.

"Then first go and get a picture clicked. I'll wait outside, otherwise everyone will freak out there," she said.

"Okay, I'll get the proof," he said.

He called Zinnia to his room on the pretext of water, got his camera and clicked a picture.

"What's this for?" she asked.

"For luck. I'm going for a very important task right now. Hope this helps," he said and left.

Rita and Aditya went to Margarita's house. Aditya introduced himself as Zinnia's fiancé to Margarita's daughter and requested her to not to tell anyone. She was a good girl at heart, so she agreed. Aditya had to take the risk of calling himself her fiancé because otherwise he felt that Margarita wouldn't help him. Her daughter was reluctant to let them meet her mother because she couldn't afford that her mother's condition deteriorates one more time. After pleading incessantly, she agreed for a short meet on the condition that she would make them leave as and when she feels that they are giving stress to her mother. They agreed and all three went inside.

Margarita freaked out on seeing them. She started shivering. Her daughter told her that Aditya was Zinnia's fiancé and had come to talk only for few minutes.

"Mom, relax. He'll just talk. I'm here. Don't worry."

Margarita calmed down a bit.

"Hello ma'am. I will not harm you in anyway. I have come here seeking your help. I love Zinnia. Her pain is mine and her sorrows too. I know what she has gone through in her past. I just don't want her to suffer more. That's why I have come here. Seeing you like this really pains me. Your daughter is very courageous. I am sure you are too. Right now, you are the only person who can help me. Or maybe, we both can help each other." Aditya took over by saying this.

Margarita's daughter asked Rita to go out lest she feels uncomfortable amongst so many people.

"Ma'am, if you don't mind, can I talk to you alone? I won't come near you. Please ma'am." He requested.

Margarita could see something in his eyes, a spark of care and honesty. She gestured her daughter to go out.

"You can keep the door open," he said.

She did the same. Afterwards, he continued, "I lost my parents at a small age, in an accident. Zinnia too doesn't have them with her. At least, I saw mine. She never saw hers. I want to help her in every way possible. I know that you knew her mother. She must have been a wonderful woman, just like her daughter. Now she lives with Mrs. Anita, the woman who is responsible for keeping her away from her parents." He bluffed the last part, based on the little information that he had.

Margarita looked at him in surprise.

His bluff worked.

"Yes, I know. I overheard her conversation with her husband. I'll be totally frank with you. I won't lie. I overheard that she was responsible for that, but I want to know more. What did she do? What had happened? Why did her father leave this town?" He continued.

Margarita started showing signs of discomfort.

"I'm sorry if I am troubling you. But Zinnia trusts Mrs. Anita very much and she doesn't treat her well in return. I heard from Mr. Hudson that she doesn't want to see Zinnia happy. I don't trust Mrs. Anita. I want to tell Zinnia the truth, but I need to know the truth first. I don't want Zinnia to hate herself because she has been told lies. She misses her father, I know. I want to know where he is. You too have a daughter, ma'am, and unfortunately she's away from her father too. We all are in the same boat. I can't bring her mother back, but maybe I can get her father back. Please help me. You may choose not to. If you don't, I'll leave and never come back here, but please know that you can help us. You knew Zinnia's mother too. For her sake, please help us." He pleaded.

He saw sorrow in Margarita's eyes.

Just when he was about to give up, he saw Margarita gesturing with her hands, asking for a pen.

He gave her a pen and sheets.

"I knew Mrs. Sabrina. She was a beautiful woman." She wrote in a handwriting which was difficult to comprehend and in her native language.

"Ma'am, I don't understand your native language. Can you write in Hindi?" he said.

She didn't respond so he took it as a no.

"Can I call your daughter or Rita to translate it for me?" he asked.

She blinked. He took it as a yes and called her daughter.

After making efforts, she could understand what her mother had written and told that to Aditya.

"I'm sure she was. Please tell me about what had Mrs. Anita done? And where did Zinnia's father go?" he said.

She wrote, while her daughter read it out loud, "He is dead. He didn't leave Sabrina."

"What? How? What had happened? Please tell me everything, I request you ma'am." He pleaded.

She wrote a few more lines. She had started feeling exhausted, but continued to write.

"My mother can't write much as of now. She has only started," her daughter said.

"I want to tell something to both of you. As I told your mom that I overheard Mrs. Anita's conversation with her husband. She was very upset that Margarita ma'am can write now. She said she would do something about this. You need to be cautious. I'll try my best to help you and arrange for your security, but please take precautions from your side," he said.

Margarita started panicking. Her daughter got scared. He calmed them down. Then, Margarita took another sheet of paper and wrote. Her daughter read out,

"Shona, save me from Anita. Every time she comes, she hurts me and stops me from recovering. She puts medicines in my mouth forcefully."

"I didn't know this happened, mom. Why didn't you tell me earlier? But how could you? You can't talk." Her daughter started crying.

"I'm responsible for all this. I should have known. My mother is in this state because of my negligence. I'll kill Mrs. Anita. I hate her. Malicious woman!" She cursed.

"Calm down. You need to think right now. Don't get carried away. Now that you know, you need to keep your mother secured. Gather as much friends like Sonam around your home as you can, and don't let Mrs. Anita get inside the house. I'll do what best I can," he said.

Margarita pointed out to the other piece of paper.

"Anita hated Sabrina. She wanted to ruin her life. Alex loved Sabrina very much. When Sabrina got pregnant, Anita wanted to kill her child. Alex got to know of her plans to poison Sabrina. He confronted her while she was going to Sabrina's house after getting the poison. It was dark. She pushed Alex. Alex was about to fall off the cliff. He resisted. He tried to snatch the poison. She didn't let it go. In all this, Anita lost her balance and was about to fall down. Alex held her and saved her from falling, but as she regained her balance, she pushed him down the cliff and he died. Sabrina couldn't believe that Alex had left her. She began investigating. Anita played very smartly. She gave her wrong medicines instead of appropriate vitamins. The investigation drained all her strength too. Her pregnancy got complicated and she died after giving birth because she was too weak." Her daughter read it out.

Everyone in the room was shocked. The entire environment turned dull and full of sadness, as if death itself had entered the room. Aditya was shattered.

"What a woman! I have never seen such a pathetic person in my entire life. And she wanted to kill a foetus! Shame on her! Please tell me how Anita knew Mrs. Sabrina?" He dropped the Mrs. from Anita.

Margarita wrote. Her hands had started shaking. Her daughter saw it, but couldn't say anything. She read out, "Sabrina was a dentist. She lived with her mother. She met Alex and married him. Her mom had a heart problem. She wasn't keeping well. Anita assisted her in dentistry. Anita didn't do her work properly. Patients got infections because she wouldn't take care of the instruments. One such patient complained about his infection to Sabrina. She warned Anita but she didn't listen. Sabrina had to bear patients' wrath, so one day she dismissed Anita from the job.

"At that time, Anita was pregnant and her family was in debt. Hudson ran a small shop. They didn't have any other source of income. Sabrina didn't know about Anita's financial crisis. Anita hadn't even announced her pregnancy till then. She pleaded to Sabrina but Sabrina knew that she wouldn't change. She couldn't see her patients suffer. After that, Anita lost her child to miscarriage while doing people's household chores. Since then, she blamed Sabrina for her misfortunes and wanted to ruin her life, which she did. Zinnia's grandmother didn't know about all this. When Sabrina died, Anita portrayed herself as a very good caretaker and won her trust. She knew that she won't live long, so they signed an agreement that after Zinnia turns eighteen, she'll get the house in her name and in the event of her grandmother's death before that, Anita can live with her family in that house provided they act as Zinnia's guardians, since Sabrina's family had nobody else."

"And what about Mr. Alex's family? They had nobody?" he asked.

"Wait. Was everyone told that he ran away? But who said that? Anita? Why did people believe her? Why did nobody try to find out? And how do you know all this?"

Margarita wrote to her daughter to go out of the room and thereafter wrote a long message for Aditya.

"I told you I can't read this. Why did you send her out? How will I understand this without her?" He was confused.

"Oh! Do you not want your daughter to read this?" he asked.

Margarita blinked.

Thereafter, she started feeling suffocated. Aditya called her daughter and kept the last sheet in his pocket.

"I told you she can't write much. I think you should go now. Please come tomorrow if you need to know more," she requested.

He asked for the rest of the sheets and kept them in the other pocket. He left the house with Rita.

On the way, he told Rita everything except the last bit because he thought that maybe it had something in it which was not to be known to everyone. Rita went to arrange for Margarita's security and Aditya went home to apprise Zinnia about the truth.

"Is Mrs. Anita home?" he asked Zinnia when he got home.

"Yes. She is with Sid." she replied.

"Tell her that you've some work outside and meet me at Harry's," he said.

"But why? What happened?" she asked.

"I'll tell you everything. Just make some excuse, and don't bring Sid along," he said with urgency in his voice.

She did as told.

Aditya knew the management pretty well since he sang at Harry's and so he demanded a private space to talk. They allowed them to go inside the Green Room where the music instruments were kept.

"Zinnia, whatever I'm going to tell you now will hurt you very much, but you need to know the truth. Please don't get so overwhelmed so as to forget fighting for what is done wrong. Be strong and fight back," he said.

"Tell me what's wrong. You're scaring me," she said.

"Do you trust me?" he asked.

"Yes, of course," she replied, "Now tell me."

He sighed. He started from the beginning. He told her how he had overheard Mrs. Anita's conversation and he had asked Rita for help, how he met Margarita and how Margarita was related to her mother.

"This is what she wrote," he said, handing over the papers to her.

With every sheet that Zinnia read, she cried even more. She was shattered. The mirage was broken. What she knew as the truth turned into a fiction to beguile her; the woman she had been living with for so many years turned into someone she never knew until then. And the woman she thought gave her a new life became the woman who had taken away everything from her and still wasn't satisfied. The world around her had changed. The person whom she had hated the most, her father, was actually the person who deserved tonnes of her love. The woman whose child was so innocent and gullible was a monster. Zinnia was struggling with herself, her past, the reality, the fake world that had been created for her, her pain, her sorrow and her anger.

"Zinnia, it's not over yet. Be strong. You have to earn justice for your parents. You can't be weak now. Use your pain as your weapon, your strength and your resolve. Don't let it become your weakness. Hate her, but in your hatred, punish her for her ever-increasing mistakes, and not yourself. Don't cry. If you cry, she'll win." He gave her courage.

"She lost her child while doing household chores, that's why she makes me do that. Isn't it?" she asked, addressing nobody in particular.

"Zinnia, I know how you feel right now. But trust me, she is responsible for everything by herself. Nobody else is," he said.

"Zinnia, read this. Margarita didn't let her daughter read it for me. I don't know what's written in this, nor have I shown it to anybody. You read it," he said, handing over the last sheet to her.

Zinnia read it and utter disgust was visible on her face.

"Tell me what's written," he said.

Zinnia read out.

"Son, I'm telling you this because you have told us that Anita knows about my improvement and is going to do something about it. I know her too well to mislead myself by thinking that I can stay alive and well. I know she wouldn't let that happen. Before I die, I want to tell the truth, to rid myself of the burden, but please don't share this with my daughter, because I don't want her to hate her mother. I was involved in the crime. I was very poor. My husband had left me when I gave birth to a daughter, and not a son. Anita gave me an offer. She said that I need to help her in her plans and in return, she'll give me money.

"Being Sabrina's help during her pregnancy, I would be with her most of the time. Anita and I made a plan to barren her. I told her about the lady who made poisons. It was me who helped her, but I didn't know she would be responsible for Sabrina's and Alex's death. His death was unforeseen. He had heard us talk at night when we were planning to get the poison. He came after us and you know what happened after that. I was too scared of Anita after that incident. I told her I couldn't help her anymore.

But she took my daughter in her custody and threatened to kill her if I didn't carry out her plans. She didn't even pay the money that was due to me and I didn't care about the money any longer. My daughter was at stake, so I had to do what she asked me to do. I wouldn't give Sabrina her vitamins.

"Together, we weakened her body. Whenever Sabrina tried to do something to find out about Alex, I would tell Anita. Together, we stopped her. I told everyone that I saw Alex leave at night and when I asked him where he was going, he said that he was going away. Sabrina had full faith in Alex. She knew that he couldn't leave her, and he didn't. When Sabrina died while giving birth, Anita freed my daughter because she didn't need me anymore. She had to gain Zinnia's grandmother's trust. But even after she asked me to leave the job, she was scared that I would blackmail her. So one day, she followed me when I had gone to a temple and pushed me down the stairs. She wanted me dead like Alex. But I survived. I was paralysed. I couldn't do anything, and till date, it has been like that. Please forgive me for my sins. I was a victim of poverty, and too helpless because she had my daughter."

Aditya was stunned. Zinnia was disgusted.

"I don't know where humanity has gone!" Aditya reacted.

"Well, I hate her too, but less than Mrs. Anita. She has paid for her sins, I guess. But it pains me to realise that I'll have to take help from someone who was the crime partner of Mrs. Anita. Anyway, we don't have any other option left. Yes, I am hurt right now and probably should be in my bed crying, but I can't waste more time. I'll have to meet her before Mrs. Anita does. Can you take me to her right now?" Zinnia said.

"Although her daughter asked me to meet her tomorrow, I'll still try. Do you want to go there this late? It's night already. We can go in the morning if you aren't comfortable," Aditya replied.

"I don't think we can take the risk, especially when we don't know what's going on in Mrs. Anita's head. She hasn't come out of her room since afternoon. I am sure she's planning something," Zinnia said.

"Did you check if she was in there?" Aditya asked after a pause.

Zinnia paused and then said, "No, I just assumed."

They both looked at each other for a minute and then Aditya said, "Run Zinnia. We need to go to Margarita before it's too late."

They both left the premises in a hurry. They headed straight to Margarita's house.

On the way, Zinnia said to Aditya, "These notes are not enough. They are confessions from a lady who's been paralysed for years, and won't be enough to punish Mrs. Anita. We need more proofs. We'll have to make Margarita speak up at any cost."

"Zinnia, tell me. Did you sign any property papers till now? Margarita mentioned the house would be in your name after you turn eighteen." Aditya asked.

"No, I haven't. I didn't even know that the house was mine," she said.

"Are you sure? You could've done it without realising," he said.

"I'm sure. Probably she didn't take the risk of getting my signature to get the house in her name because she feared that I'll read them or get to know about it. She would've been caught then," she replied.

"Yes. It can be that. Plus, she would've thought that it would be better to not take any risk because anyway you would've never known all this," he said.

Soon, they reached Margarita's house. They could see Sonam sitting outside the house.

Sonam saw Zinnia and recognised her.

"Zinnia, what are you doing here? And who are you?" She addressed Zinnia and Aditya.

"He's Aditya, the love of my life," Zinnia answered.

Aditya couldn't believe his ears. Zinnia had confessed her love to Sonam, without hesitating a bit. She wasn't scared of people knowing anymore. She said it with such pride.

"I'm Sonam. Why have you come here?" Sonam replied.

"Oh! So you're Sonam! Rita told me about you. We are your friends, don't worry. We have come here to meet Margarita." Aditya assured her of their intentions.

"I'm sorry, but she isn't well. You can't meet her right now," she said.

Hearing them talk, Margarita's daughter came outside.

"Hey, is everything fine here? Did Mrs. Anita visit you? Have you arranged for security? Did Rita come back?" Aditya hurled questions at her.

"Mrs. Anita hasn't visited yet. We have two more ladies inside to not let anybody in. Rita hasn't come back yet," she answered.

She looked at Zinnia.

"Hi. I'm Zinnia. I understand that your mother isn't well. But she's the only person who can help me. I don't have much time. I have waited too long to know about my parents. Aditya told me that you asked him to come tomorrow, but meeting her right now is very important for me. I'll just take a few minutes." Zinnia pleaded.

"I understand that you've lost your parents. But try to understand that she's my mother. Meeting you can cause her condition to deteriorate further. I can't afford to lose her," she replied.

"I won't meet her without her consent. We'll wait here. You can go inside and ask her if she would like to see me. If she says no, we'll leave. I hope you can do that much?" Zinnia replied.

She agreed. She went inside and after a minute, allowed them to get in.

Zinnia and Aditya went inside Margarita's room.

Margarita stared at Zinnia without panicking. Zinnia sat down beside her and said, "Margarita, I have read your notes. After a long time, I am meeting someone other than Mrs. Anita who was close to my mother in some way. Honestly, I hated you after reading your confession, but also thought that you've paid for your sins. Now seeing you in this state has made me feel bad for you. I'll forgive you if you help us," she said.

Margarita looked at her helplessly.

"I want to punish Mrs. Anita for her sins. For that, I need your help. Please tell me if you know of any proof that can work against her. I promise you that your name won't come in between and we'll protect you from her," she said.

Aditya put a pen and sheets near her. Margarita didn't write anything.

"Let's start with describing my parents. Tell me how they were?" Zinnia asked.

Aditya put his hand over her shoulder.

Margarita wrote. Zinnia read silently.

"Your mother was very beautiful, just like you. In fact, you look just like her. She was a woman with dignity and everyone respected her for her work. She was a reputed dentist but her reputation suffered because patients caught infections due to Anita's negligence. Your father was courageous. He was a handsome man. He loved Sabrina very much. Whenever something troubled her, he would take it in his hand to resolve it. Sabrina trusted Alex more than herself. For her, Alex meant the world."

Zinnia longed to see her parents.

"Do you have their photograph?" she asked.

"No." She wrote.

"Okay. Now tell me if there's any proof? Please think about everything. Tell me, if there's even the smallest detail that you might not have mentioned yet," Zinnia asked.

Margarita kept silent.

"Please Margarita. Don't you want to help me?" Zinnia asked.

Margarita began writing. Aditya heard some noise outside. He went out to check. He saw nobody except Sonam and Margarita's daughter, so he came back after asking where the rest of them had gone. "Home," they replied.

"When Anita and I buried Alex that night after locating where he had fallen down, I got my hands on the watch that he had with him. The watch was expensive and not from here. His name, Alex Daniels, was embossed on it. While Anita was putting him in the grave which she had dug for him, I saw his name on the watch. Mrs. Anita had asked me to throw the watch somewhere so that nobody recognises his body by the watch.

Instead of throwing it away, I buried it near the body when she wasn't looking. I didn't go back there. Neither did I tell Anita that I had buried the watch there. I told her that I threw it in the valley. You can go and check if it's still there."

"Where's that place?" Zinnia asked.

"Near the town graveyard." She wrote.

"Exactly where?" she asked further.

Margarita wrote the exact location.

"Zinnia, what's happening?" Aditya asked.

"I've found a proof. My dad's watch with his name embossed on it, buried near his body," she answered.

"Thank you Margarita. Is there anything else you can tell us?" she asked.

Margarita's daughter rushed inside the room.

"What was Mrs. Anita doing here? Where's Sonam?" she asked in one breath.

"What? Where? Where did you see her?" Aditya asked.

"Here. I saw her running outside the house. She must have been standing at the door. I had gone to the kitchen," she said.

"Oh my god! Zinnia, she must have heard all this. We need to find the watch before she does," Aditya said.

They ran outside the house. They took a cab. Zinnia told the driver the address.

"How fast does Mrs. Anita drive?" Aditya asked Zinnia.

"Pretty fast!" she replied.

They were worried.

"Drive fast!" Aditya addressed the driver.

He called Rita and asked her to reach Margarita's house as soon as possible, for Margarita's safety.

Karma

"Gentleman, please be fast," Zinnia said.

"It is night already. I am driving as fast as I can without compromising on security, madam," the driver replied.

"Relax Zinnia. Everything is under control. I am sure she mustn't be over speeding her car that much because these roads are risky, especially at night," Aditya said, trying to make Zinnia feel better.

"More than anything that I am concerned about, I pity myself because I couldn't even save my father's last memory," said Zinnia.

"Don't lose hope yet, Zinnia. We're going at good speed. We won't let her slip away," Aditya tried to calm her.

On the other hand, Mrs. Anita was driving as fast as she could. She had already called Mr. Hudson and asked him to reach the cemetery on urgent basis.

It was dark. The roads were dangerous. Mrs. Anita's car took sharp turns. Driving was getting difficult.

When Aditya and Zinnia reached the place, Mrs. Anita had dug out the watch. She knew where Alex was buried, so she had a better idea of where the watch could be. In addition to that, she knew where Margarita was standing that night, when they were in the graveyard.

Nothing worked for Aditya and Zinnia that night. The cab driver took a cautious and secure approach, and the place wasn't easy to find either. Whereas, Mrs. Anita had rushed to the cemetery as soon as she heard Zinnia talking about that watch. All this gave Mrs. Anita an upper hand, and by the time they reached, Mrs. Anita was rushing out after locating the watch.

"Wait for us. We'll pay you double." Aditya told the cab driver.

"Finding that watch would be really difficult at this time," Zinnia said on reaching the place.

"Do keep an eye for Anita. She must be around here," Aditya replied.

"Can you hear that? There's someone running. Can you hear footsteps churning dead leaves?" Aditya asked.

"Yes," Zinnia replied.

Both of them ran towards the gate.

"There she is!" Aditya shouted on seeing Mrs. Anita run.

Aditya and Zinnia ran as fast as they could.

"Stop! Stop! You've been caught!" Zinnia shouted from behind.

Mrs. Anita looked behind. She saw them. Zinnia was way behind Aditya. Aditya ran like a leopard and caught Mrs. Anita while she was trying to sit in the car.

He pulled her out.

They were on the road now.

"Stay away from me!" Mrs. Anita shouted.

"Help! Help!" She shouted again.

Aditya put his hands on her mouth. Zinnia reached the point where they stood.

"Give me the watch!" she said, trying to snatch the watch from Mrs. Anita.

After much resistance, Aditya held Mrs. Anita's arms. She hit him in the groin and pushed him away.

Zinnia jumped to get the watch.

They had reached the end of the road now. There were no barricades there. Zinnia and Mrs. Anita fought. They both resisted. They battled with each other for a minute. Mrs. Anita pulled her hands out. She threatened Zinnia that she would drop the watch, and since it was the end of the road, Zinnia would never get that watch once it went down in the valley.

Aditya was back on his feet by then. As soon as Mrs. Anita saw him coming, she pushed Zinnia with all her force and threw the watch away.

"No!" Zinnia shouted.

Mrs. Anita pushed Zinnia one more time to make her lose her balance so that she falls down the valley, but Aditya held her.

"Zinnia!" He shouted while saving her.

Mrs. Anita ran towards her car.

Aditya and Zinnia ran towards their cab.

"Follow her!" Aditya ordered the cab driver.

Mrs. Anita drove as fast as she could.

"What if they locate the watch? I have to tell Hudson to do it. But where would it have fallen? I don't think anybody can ever locate that watch now. But what if they do? But how would Hudson locate it? It's dark. I don't think Zinnia would be capable enough to get to that watch! Plus, the slope is too steep. Anybody who goes down would risk his life. Nobody can go down. There's no way. The watch is gone for good. But where is Hudson? He was supposed to come to the cemetery!" Mrs. Anita was talking to herself in stress.

A zillion thoughts had crossed her mind while driving.

"Aditya, we won't ever find that watch again. That was the last memory I could've had of my parents. Isn't there a way? Please tell me there is," cried Zinnia.

"Zinnia, the watch fell down in the valley. We can't possibly get it back again," he replied.

Zinnia started crying louder. Aditya hugged her.

"I know it's hurting very badly, Zinnia. I know how it feels. Nothing can take away your pain right now, I know. But that's the truth. There's nothing we can do about it, except facing it together." He consoled her.

He pulled up her face by her chin. Her tears gushed forth. He hugged her even tighter. He noticed that Mrs. Anita was still driving pretty fast.

"The watch is gone, then why is she driving that fast? There's no reason why she should be scared of us to drive away that fast. What's going on in her head?" Aditya thought.

Suddenly a thought struck him and he immediately took out his phone to call Rita.

"Rita, you guys need to be careful. Mrs. Anita is coming for Margarita. I am sure she won't let her live because she is the only one left to prove her guilt. She won't take that risk. Gather as much security as you can. Call the cops. We're coming," he said.

Rita cut the call in a hurry and called out to Margarita's daughter to inform her of the same.

Back in her car, Mrs. Anita thought, "I won't spare Margarita. She has backstabbed me. If she doesn't live, nobody can prove anything. I'll end her suffering today for good. But how do I go unnoticed and still cause her death? I'll have to call Hudson."

Suddenly, her phone rang.

She struggled to take out the phone from the pocket.

She narrowly missed hitting a car on a sharp turn since it was too dark and she was too fast for mountain roads. The area was such that there were no barricades to mark the roads, and the blind turns made it difficult to judge the traffic coming from the other end.

As soon as she took out the phone, a car appeared in the front when she reached the turn.

Her hands fumbled and the phone slipped away.

"Gosh! Where is the phone now? I'll have to find it." She murmured.

She began searching for her phone below the seats, while driving with her right hand and searching with her left. Her eyeballs took turns to look towards the road and the floor of the car.

She didn't realise when she had almost reached a turn.

"Here it is!" She murmured. "Hello," she said on picking up the call.

"Hello," Mr. Hudson replied.

Suddenly, she saw a car coming at a high speed from the other side. She shouted and moved her steering wheel towards the left.

"What's wrong?" Mr. Hudson shouted from the other side.

She couldn't control her speed, and in the blink of an eye, her car understeered and crashed down into the drench as there were no barricades.

There was a loud noise. The car caught fire, after rolling down the drench. The call got disconnected. At the surface where the drench ended, it exploded. Flashes of light illuminated the otherwise darkest spot of the area.

"What happened?" Zinnia shouted.

"Stop the car!" Aditya called out the driver.

They got off the car and saw Mrs. Anita's car burning into flames.

Zinnia couldn't bear it and fainted. Aditya held her.

"Zinnia! Zinnia! Open your eyes!" He shouted.

Zinnia's vision kept blurring. She couldn't hear Aditya any longer.

Aditya took Zinnia back in the car and called Mr. Hudson.

When Zinnia opened her eyes, she was lying on Aditya's bed.

"Zinnia, are you okay?" Aditya asked, sitting beside her and caressing her face.

"Mrs. Anita?" Zinnia asked back.

"She's gone," Aditya replied with his face down.

"Sid? Where is he? How is he? Sid! Sid!" Zinnia started shouting in hurry.

"Zinnia! Zinnia! Lie down. Sid is sleeping. Mr. Hudson hasn't told him anything yet," Aditya said, trying to calm her.

Zinnia started crying loudly. All the pain that she had kept inside her, had found its catharsis.

Zinnia had seen three people die that day. She came to know about the truth behind her parents' death and lost the person who was responsible for their death. It was a tragic day for Zinnia and she wished nothing had ever happened. Her entire world was shaken in one single day. Her entire life had become a façade. She was taken aback. She cursed her stars. She cursed her life. She was too overwhelmed. She never wanted Mrs. Anita to die. She wanted to punish her, but not at the cost of hurting Sid. Ironically, punishing the person who killed her parents required her to hurt the one person she had been living for all along – Sid.

Aditya could feel the excruciating pain that Zinnia was experiencing. He could feel the pain hidden in her loudest cry, the meaninglessness behind her quietest sob and the disbelief in the little breaths she took in between her sobbing. Aditya knew that it was her weakest moment. He not only held her hand, but could also capture the increasing pace of her heartbeat through her pulse. He knew when her heart rate was increasing and when it almost stopped. He could read the thoughts in her head through her face, the tears and her restlessness. But he could do nothing about it. He couldn't mitigate the pain. Zinnia had to go through it. Realising his helplessness in terms of doing something, he decided to be a quiet companion in this journey, who would never let her fall.

"Sid won't be able to take it. How would he react? Would he hate me for it? Tell me, Aditya, would he?" Zinnia started panicking.

"No. You are not at fault in this. She wasn't over-speeding because she was scared of us. She wanted to harm Margarita to save her own skin, after all that she had done in the past, but it all came down on her. She wasn't even guilty about what she had done. She was being selfish. She was thinking about saving herself at the cost of others. In all these years, she hadn't changed a bit." Aditya made her accept the truth.

"Don't blame yourself Zinnia. You, your parents, Sid – you're all victims. The victims of someone else's deeds," Aditya consoled her.

"Aditya, I can't take all this. I feel weak. I want to run away. I want to die. I can't…," Zinnia gave up in his arms.

"I'm with you Zinnia. You're not alone." Aditya kissed her on the forehead. He put his hands inside her hair, and caressed her the entire night.

In the morning, Mr. Hudson came to see Zinnia. Aditya told him everything.

"I know it. I was on the phone when her car…," he couldn't speak more.

"But it had to happen one day. She always chose the wrong path. I knew Karma would strike her one day. I tried to make her understand, but she couldn't help being mean. She thought only of herself," he said.

"When will you tell Sid about all this?" Aditya asked.

"I don't have the courage," he said and went away.

A week had passed since Mrs. Anita's death. Zinnia hadn't spoken much since then. Aditya would force her to eat. He never left her side. He remained with her the entire day. Zinnia would cook, but lifelessly. She would do nothing apart from cooking meals. She did that for Sid because Sid loved what she cooked. Aditya would accompany her to the kitchen and cook with her. She didn't talk about anything except food.

Aditya would keep her in his arms all day. He calmed her when she cried, supported her body when she fell asleep and made her eat her food.

Sid had come to know about his mother's death. He would remain with Mr. Hudson the entire day. Zinnia avoided confronting him. He was told that his mother died in an accident, but not the story behind it.

"Zinnia, Sid needs you. Please start spending time with him," Aditya said.

"I can't face him," she said.

"It's not your fault, Zinnia. Why don't you understand?" Aditya replied.

"Why are you punishing Sid for what his mother did? By blaming yourself for hurting Sid, you're not only punishing yourself, but also him," he added.

"Sid is just a kid. Would you want Sid to live like you did in your childhood? He needs a mother just like you did. He needs your love," he continued.

"I know that, Aditya. I know everything. But I can't face my own reflection. I'm too weak. How do I make him feel alright when I myself don't feel that way? I'm too broken to support anyone," she replied.

She started crying soon after.

"No, you're not weak. You are strong. Just like your mother. You know what she did after your father died, don't you? Did she lay wasted or did she fight back? She fought back, Zinnia. She made efforts. She turned her weakness into her strength. You've to do just that." Aditya tried to encourage her, thinking maybe he shouldn't have used her mother's fight as an example.

Zinnia looked at him for a minute. She looked right into his eyes and heard his words echoing in her ears.

"Are we completing their story which they left unfinished?" she asked.

"Yes," he replied.

From that moment, Zinnia never looked back. She gave Sid courage to face the world. She made him smile, play, eat and live his life again. In that process, she rediscovered herself too. Their life had started getting back to normal. Slowly, the pain was going away. Aditya, Mr. Hudson and Rita supported Zinnia and Sid to the fullest. They were recovering slowly.

Three months had passed. Aditya had been by Zinnia's side the entire time. In order to make her feel normal again, they talked about all sorts of places, things and cultures. They talked about astronomy, astrology, psychology and literature. They talked about ideas, books and characters. They discovered themselves and each other in such discussions. Their favourite books and characters told them a lot about each other.

Looking at the stars at night together made them acknowledge how badly they wanted to do it for the rest of their lives, together. Talking about places made them feel the warmth that was between them, as all the places they talked about were the ones they wanted to visit together. Their shared interests, their conflicting opinions, the sweet nothings, the bitter truths, the hard times, the happy events, the memories, the broken dreams and the unbroken promises heightened their love to a new level, the level which they both were unaware of. They had become each other's shadow and even more than that, the true companions who would never part, not even in darkness.

"Zinnia, it's your house. Although Anita had got false papers made just in case you ever asked about it, still it would remain yours. Sid and I would shift somewhere else, if you want," Mr. Hudson said one day.

"No, Mr. Hudson. This house belongs to my family, and you are my family. You don't need to go anywhere. You and Sid would live here forever," she said.

Meanwhile, Sid had been playing with Aditya.

"Uncle, you said you had visited places," he said.

"Yes, I did." Aditya replied.

"But now you don't go anywhere?" he asked.

"Do you want me to go?" Aditya asked back.

"No, no… Zinnia told me that visiting new places is your life. Then why don't you live your life now?" he asked.

"You've grown up, little kid. Huh?" Aditya said.

"You should live your life because you never know when it will end." The young boy continued.

"I will," Aditya said, getting up.

"But I don't want to go anywhere alone now," he added.

"Then take Zinnia along," he said smiling.

"And you?" Aditya asked.

"I'm too small right now. I will join you when I grow up," he said.

"And who would take care of you meanwhile?" Aditya asked.

"Dad," he replied.

"I'll go later, kid. It can wait," Aditya replied.

The young boy thought that it would be best to talk to Zinnia about it. So at night, he went to Zinnia.

"Why don't you accompany Aditya uncle?"

"Accompany him where?" she asked back.

"To new places," he replied.

Zinnia kept quiet.

"You said it was his life. So why is he not living it now?" he asked.

Zinnia had no answer.

"We'll talk about it tomorrow. Go sleep now. It's very late," she said.

Sid did as instructed. They exchanged good night kisses after which Sid went to his room. But the little boy had said much in his innocence without realising. He had made Zinnia realise how much Aditya had been sacrificing. He had shown her the way.

She immediately went to see Aditya who wasn't in his room. She went to the gallery and found him there.

"What are you doing here?" she asked.

"Getting fresh air," he replied.

"You've done so much for me without thinking about yourself. You left everything you like, just to be with me. You didn't step out of the house, just to take care of me. You stopped visiting places, just to be with me. You just made it feel so natural, this way of living at one place," she said.

"It didn't feel like it took any effort, because it didn't. Doing something for you doesn't need any effort. Now, I live by doing things for you. I live for you," he said.

She came closer, caressed his face with her hands and said, "Now, let me live for you. Let me complete my parents' story."

She took his hands in hers and asked, "Would you be a traveller for me again? Would you pack our bags and take me somewhere you've always wanted to go? Would you travel the world with me?"

Aditya couldn't control his emotions. He was overwhelmed to hear those words from Zinnia.

"Of course. You and only you. Always," he replied.

They hugged each other passionately.

Aditya lifted her up until her lips landed on his, and kissed her. They kissed as if it was the union of two lost souls.

That moment marked the beginning of a new life for both of them to get the happiness they truly deserved.

"Tell me where do you want to go first?" Aditya asked.

"The place which made me realise that I have feelings for you," she said.

"Sikkim," she said after a pause.

And together, they travelled the world, after saying their good-byes to everyone. Zinnia promised Sid and Rita that they would meet them every year and would stay in touch.

Zinnia and Aditya started off with Sikkim, after bidding farewell to their friends, Rita and Mr. John, and went on to chart out the paths less trodden. It was destiny which made them meet and love which kept them together. Together, they lived a life of their choice and gave companionship a new meaning, to complete a story that was left unfinished decades ago.